The Mad Hacker

Susan Brown   **Anne Stephenson**

Scholastic Canada Ltd.

The Amber and Elliot Mysteries:

The Mad Hacker
Something's Fishy at Ash Lake

Other books by Susan Brown:

Not Yet Summer
Hey, Chicken Man

Other books by Anne Stephenson:

The Mysterious Mr. Moon (General Publishing)
Paper Treasure (General Publishing)

To Bobby, Brian, Matthew, Laurel, Lindsay,
Heather and Karen
With Love

Scholastic Canada Ltd.
123 Newkirk Road, Richmond Hill, Ontario, Canada L4C 3G5

Scholastic Inc.
730 Broadway, New York, NY 10003, USA

Ashton Scholastic Pty Limited
PO Box 579, Gosford, NSW 2250, Australia

Ashton Scholastic Limited
Private Bag 1, Penrose, Auckland, New Zealand

Scholastic Publications Ltd.
Villiers House, Clarendon Avenue, Leamington Spa, Warwickshire
CV32 5PR, UK

Canadian Cataloguing in Publication Data

Brown, Susan
    The Mad Hacker

ISBN-0590-71388-4

I. Stephenson, Anne. II. Title.

PS8553.R6886M32 1987   jC813'.54   C87-093612-3
PZ7.B766Ma 1987

6 5 4 3 2   Printed in Canada   3 4 5 6 7/9
                    Manufactured by Webcom Limited

Contents

Chapter 1
Doom and destruction

The halls of Ash Grove Junior High should have been deserted as the students settled into the last class of the day. Instead, they echoed with racing footsteps. Amber Mitchell and Liz Elliot had business to attend to.

"You do the talking," Liz urged as they stopped just short of their destination. "Teachers make me nervous. You're better at talking to Jaws than I am. I think I'll just wait out here." She leaned casually against the wall.

"Chicken!" Amber teased. Teachers didn't faze her one bit.

"Discreet," countered Liz. She wound a strand of long, dark hair around and around one finger. "Go for it! Our future is in your hands."

"Gee, thanks. Here goes nothing!" Amber inhaled deeply, tossed her copper-red hair, and resolutely walked into the classroom. Mr. Eugene Sharkman, better known as Jaws, was busy at the blackboard, writing out assignments for his next day's computer science classes.

"Excuse me, sir."

"What? Oh, Amber. What can I do for you?"

Chalk in hand, Mr. Sharkman peered at her over his wire-rimmed glasses.

"Liz and I were wondering if we could have some extra time on the Abacus computers to test our *Whodunnit* program."

"Ah, yes. That video mystery game. Why? Are you having a problem?"

"Yes. It's Aunt Agatha. She keeps killing the butler. Over and over again. With the knife in the parlour, the rope in the kitchen, the machete in the bedroom . . . "

"She sounds like she is a problem." His mouth twitched with amusement.

"Yes sir," Amber answered, freckles blending into one big blush. "But Jonathan Weiss told us how to fix it . . . if we could have just one more hour on the computer?"

"I suppose that can be arranged," answered her teacher, checking the logbook on his desk. "But just this once. You know our agreement with Eastern Technology is for normal class work only. How would four o'clock be?"

"That's great, sir. Thanks."

Elated by her success, Amber raced out of the room.

"We've got it! We can use the Abacus for an hour after school today."

"Thank goodness," Liz said. "I hope *Whodunnit* runs smoothly this time. I lie awake at night worrying about that poor butler."

"Right. We'll get an F on our project and I'll be grounded for a thousand years, but he'll make the *Guiness Book of World Records* — the only butler who didn't do it."

"Very funny, Amber."

"I thought so."

Liz looked at her watch.

"We'd better hurry. We're already ten minutes late for gym."

The girls started running down the empty hall toward their next class. Suddenly a high screech echoed from behind.

"Amber Mitchell! Liz Elliot! Stop right there!"

The girls skidded to a halt.

"Oh no!" whispered Amber. "Why is it always Miss Belcher! If we get a detention after school, we're finished. Jaws will never give us another chance."

"Well, think of an excuse quick," urged Liz as she looked back over her shoulder. "Here comes the dragon lady, and I see smoke coming out of her nostrils."

"Ladies — and I use the term loosely," cried Miss Belcher as she drew level with the girls, "we walk in the halls of Ash Grove. This is the second time today I've had to remind you." She stretched her tall frame to even greater heights and fixed the two offenders with one of her most withering stares. "Must I give you a detention to implant that in your minds?"

"Miss Belcher, you can't," Liz protested.

"It's not our fault," Amber pleaded.

"Is is ever?"

"No . . . I mean," Amber stammered, "You see Jaws — I mean Mr. Sharkman — met us between classes to discuss our term project, and

3

we were late, so he told us to hurry to our next class." She smiled winningly.

"Oh?" replied Miss Belcher. "Somehow I doubt Mr. Sharkman intended for you to run to your next class. However, I'll let it go — this time. But I'd walk if I were you. From now on, I'll be watching."

"Yes, Miss Belcher," Amber said, still smiling.

"Thank you, Miss Belcher," Liz added.

They solemnly turned and walked down the hall, avoiding each others' eyes. But once they rounded the corner to the gym, they collapsed against the wall.

"Amber," Liz asked. "Why us?"

Amber grinned. "Just lucky I guess."

*   *   *

With the ease of much practice (it happened that they were late at least once a week), Liz and Amber changed into shorts and T-shirts, slipped into the gym, and joined a queue of kids at the trampoline.

"Where have you been?" demanded Jane Dobbs, the class motor-mouth. As usual, not a strand of her straight hair was out of place, and her gym clothes looked like she'd spent hours pressing them. "First Craig Nicholson takes off to see the nurse on some phony excuse, and then you two cruise in fifteen minutes late. This isn't a school, it's a zoo."

"And you're the star attraction," muttered Amber as she bent down to tie her gym shoes.

"We were begging Jaws for more time on our

term project," admitted Liz. Painful experience had taught her that it was better to give Jane a little information than none at all. Her tongue could be wicked.

"Did you get it?"

"One more hour on the Abacus. Today, after school."

"Hmph," sniffed Jane. "I'd sure like to know what you two are working on. What's the big secret?"

"You'll see Friday," Amber snapped.

Liz jabbed her friend in the ribs.

"You hope. Move it, Jane. It's your turn."

*   *   *

Thirty minutes later, once again dressed in their regular clothes, Amber and Liz hurried up the stairs to the school's second floor.

"Hold it," Amber said as Liz turned in the direction of the computer room. "We'd better ask Geoffrey to let Mom know I'll be late." Geoffrey was Amber's fourteen-year-old brother, generally known among the girls of the school as the cutest guy in eighth grade. Amber couldn't see it.

"Why not phone, like I did?" Liz had firm orders to call the family housekeeper if she was delayed after school.

Amber grinned. "Because you don't have five-year-old twin brothers who fight over the telephone and then garble the message. If he remembers, Geoff will at least get it straight."

As usual, Geoffrey was joking around with a couple of his friends beside his locker.

"Hi, Geoffrey," Liz said, and blushed.

"Hey, Geoffrey, do me a favour and tell Mom I won't be home until after five, okay?" Amber asked.

"What's up?" demanded Geoffrey. "You two get another detention? There was a gleam in the dragon lady's eye."

"We are model students," Amber said theatrically.

"Sure."

"Actually, Jaws gave us an extra hour on the Abacus," Liz explained, "for our project."

"The famous secret project," Geoff interrupted, grinning at his buddies. "Don't press any wrong keys. You two could screw up the whole school. Doom and destruction await you in the computer room . . . " He hunched his shoulders and laughed maniacally.

Liz stepped back.

"Ignore him, Liz," Amber advised. "He's been watching too many old monster movies on TV. He senses kindred spirits."

"Take a hike," replied Geoffrey.

The girls laughed and ran down the hall toward the computer room, nearly colliding with another student as they turned in the door.

"Hey, Jonathan! What are you doing here?" Amber asked.

"I . . . uh . . . I just forgot something," Jonathan stammered, colouring to the roots of his dark hair. "Besides, I could ask you the same question."

"Do you want to watch us test-run *Whodunnit*? Jaws said we could use the computers after school," replied Liz. "We're going to make those changes you suggested."

"No, I can't. I've got to go." He took off rapidly down the stairs.

"Wow! He's really acting weird," Liz said.

"No kidding," agreed Amber. "Geoffrey says he hardly hangs around with the guys any more. I think he's taking his parents' divorce pretty hard."

"He must be," agreed Liz. "He wasn't even interested in Aunt Agatha."

"Definitely not normal."

"He shouldn't have been in here, you know," Liz said as they went into the computer room. "The grade eight class finished their projects last week."

"And if we don't put a lid on Aunt Agatha, we aren't ever going to finish. If I don't get an A from Jaws, I won't survive the D I'll get from Miss Belcher."

She sat down at the keyboard of the Abacus, while Liz passed her one of the small, black disks supplied by Eastern Technology. Amber loaded it into the disk drive and keyed in their program name. Their project was stored on the disk along with a dozen others from their class.

"That's strange," Amber said after a minute. "I can't retrieve the program."

"Maybe you hit a wrong key. You've done it before." Liz sat forward in her chair to peer at the monitor.

"No, I don't think I did . . ."

Amber frowned, cleared her commands, and began again. Liz idly looked over the printout from their previous run. The other kids might be satisfied with word and number games, but true to form, Liz and Amber had gotten carried away with the possibilities. Characters, murder weapons, and motives. The player was supposed to discover "whodunnit." The trouble was, Aunt Agatha kept doing it.

"Something's wrong, Liz," Amber said. Her voice had an edge to it. Startled, Liz looked at the words flashing across the screen:

PROGRAM NOT FOUND

"Amber, what's happened?"

"It's gone," Amber said tightly. "The whole thing is gone. Our program has been erased."

The girls looked at each other then back at the flashing screen.

"Jaws is going to eat us alive!"

Chapter 2
"How strange!"

"Don't panic!" said Amber. She stared at the flashing monitor. "It's probably some little glitch. We'll just do it again, carefully, step by step."

But still the monitor flashed:

PROGRAM NOT FOUND

"I knew it," Liz said. "I knew something would go wrong. We were going to impress the whole school with *Whodunnit*, and now look at us. We can't even find it!"

"There has to be a logical explanation . . ." began Amber. "But what?" Her eyes never left the screen. "It's no use. We'll have to tell Jaws," she concluded gloomily.

"Why do these things always happen to us?" moaned Liz, slumping back in her chair. Suddenly she bounced forward again. "Wait a minute! Remember Jane carrying on about the name Lindsay and Heather picked for their program?"

"Yes. So what?"

"Maybe the same thing has happened to everyone else!"

"And so we didn't mess up after all," Amber reasoned. "Quick! Tell me the name!"

"Are you ready for this? *Barf-it*."

"What?"

"*Barf-it.*"

"That's gross!" Shaking her head, Amber keyed in the program name. The two girls hovered anxiously over the monitor. The same words flashed again:

PROGRAM NOT FOUND

"So it wasn't us," Amber sighed.

"I knew it," Liz agreed. "That's what the school gets for using an experimental computer. The Abacus has finally flipped out. We'd better find Jaws. This is more than we can handle."

*   *   *

"You girls looking for something?" demanded an unexpected voice as the girls barged into Mr. Sharkman's classroom. The school custodian, Chester Mallory, straightened up from behind the teacher's desk. His scowl seemed to fill his whole face, right up to the thinning line of his brown hair.

"We're looking for Mr. Sharkman," Liz said.

"He isn't here."

"Do you know where he is?" asked Amber.

"I've got enough to do around here, cleaning up after you kids without keeping track of the teachers." He turned and reached for his broom.

Amber snorted.

"Come on, Amber. Let's try the staff room," Liz urged, grabbing her friend's arm and pivoting her toward the door. "And watch your mouth," she added under her breath. "The last thing we need is more trouble."

10

Mr. Eugene Sharkman, his glasses perched precariously on the end of his nose, was reclining in the staff room's only easy chair enjoying the latest issue of *Technology for Teachers*. This was his favourite time of day. Everyone had gone home; the rooms and hallways were quiet save for the distant swish, swish of Mr. Mallory's broom and the faraway voices drifting in the window from the football field.

"Mr. Sharkman."

"What?" Mr. Sharkman jumped in the chair, his magazine falling to the floor. "Oh, Miss Belcher!"

"I'm so glad I caught you. I want to talk to you about two of your homeroom students, Liz Elliot and Amber Mitchell."

"Oh?" Mr. Sharkman replied cautiously. "What now? They're not organizing another fund-raiser I hope. I'm still recovering from last month's pancake breakfast."

Miss Belcher chortled. "They were the worst pancakes I ever tasted."

"So what are they up to this time?"

"Just the usual — running in the halls, late for class, improbable excuses."

"I gather you want me to have one of my famous little chats with them."

"You've got your image; I've got mine."

"Very true." Mr. Sharkman stood up and retrieved his magazine from the floor. "They're working in the computer room right now. I could . . ."

The door flew open.

"Mr. Sharkman!" exclaimed Liz.

"Hello girls. I was just coming to see how you're getting along."

"Not very well actually," said Amber breathlessly. "We've run into a problem. We can't retrieve our program."

"And we can't find anyone else's either," put in Liz. "The Abacus keeps flashing 'program not found' whenever we try to load our project."

"How strange," replied Mr. Sharkman, handing his magazine to Miss Belcher and reaching for his inevitable plaid jacket. "This should not be. Follow me, girls. We'll investigate."

He strode out of the room, leaving Miss Belcher shaking her head in disbelief.

"Keep me posted, Eugene," she called out after him.

"*Eugene*?" Liz whispered.

Amber stifled a giggle.

They fell in behind Mr. Sharkman.

"I wonder if Jonathan knows anything about the missing programs?" Liz whispered to Amber.

"He sure acted strange when he came out of the computer room," Amber had to admit.

They didn't notice Chester Mallory pushing his broom just outside the staff room door. He'd heard every word.

* * *

"Now, let's see what this is all about," said Mr. Sharkman, lowering himself into the chair Amber had vacated a few minutes before. "What's the name of your program again . . . *Whodunnit*?"

12

"Yes," Liz said. "W-H-O-D-U-N-N-I-T."

Jaws placed his long knobby fingers on the Abacus and keyed in the necessary commands. The results were the same:

PROGRAM NOT FOUND

"How strange," he murmured. "Are you sure that's the correct spelling?"

"Yes sir," Liz replied. "That's it."

"Hmm . . . And what makes you think your classmates are having the same problem?"

"We knew someone else's program name, so we tried it," explained Amber.

"And it is?"

Silence. Mr. Sharkman looked up from the screen.

"Girls?"

"Uh, we'd rather not say, sir," replied Liz. She shifted from one foot to the other and looked to Amber in silent appeal.

"Come on, girls. You're wasting time," admonished Jaws.

"It's *Barf-it*, sir," mumbled Liz. Amber stared thoughtfully at the ceiling. Liz scrutinized the floor.

"What did you say?"

"*Barf-it*, sir."

"What kind of program is that?" Jaws shook his head and turned back to the keyboard. "I can't wait to see these projects," he said under his breath as he entered the name.

"How strange!" he said again as the now familiar message appeared. "It seems, girls, that we have a problem on our hands!"

*   *   *

"I'm home," yelled Amber, as the screen door slapped shut behind her.

"Just in time for dinner," answered her mother from the kitchen. "Wash up, and then you can tell me why you're so late. I was about to send Geoffrey looking for you."

"Sorry, Mom." Amber hung her knapsack in the hall closet, then threaded her way expertly past the sprawled twins and their scattered belongings on the family room floor. "I couldn't help being late," she called. "You won't believe what's happened."

"Tell me at the table. Come on boys, tidy up. Five minutes before dinner is served. Call Geoffrey and your father, please."

Timmy and Tommy ignored the tidy up order, but careered around the house, loudly summoning Geoffrey from his attic bedroom and their father from the basement laundry room.

"Are we all here?" Dr. Mitchell asked a few minutes later as he sat down at the table. As always, he looked slightly rumpled and his hair was a mess. And as always, dinner began with his asking if they were all there . . .

"So," began Mrs. Mitchell as she dexterously intercepted Tommy's grab for the butter, "what was the problem at school, Amber? Geoffrey said you and Liz were doing extra work on your project for Mr. Sharkman."

"Is that Jaws?" asked Timmy. "No peas. Yucko!" He glared as his father served him a small portion.

"What does he look like?" demanded Tommy. "Big teeth?" He snapped menacingly at Amber.

"Creep," Amber whispered.

"A shark in a plaid sports jacket," answered Geoffrey. He grinned at Amber as he heaped potatoes onto his plate.

"Don't egg your brothers on," advised his father. "The last thing these two need is encouragement."

"Now Amber," Mrs. Mitchell smiled wryly, "what were you trying to tell us?"

"It's our computer game. Aunt Agatha keeps killing the butler, so Mr. Sharkman gave us some extra time on the Abacus today after school."

"Who's Aunt Agatha?" asked Timmy.

"Amber," Tommy eyed his sister seriously, "shouldn't you call the police?"

"No, boys. It's only a game," said Dr. Mitchell.

"It *was* a game," Amber said. "When we tried to load it this afternoon, the Abacus said it was gone."

Geoffrey frowned. "Are you sure?"

"Yes. But what's really weird is that the same thing has happened to the whole class."

"The whole class! Does Jaws know?" Geoffrey stopped eating to stare at her.

Amber nodded. "We told him the name of another program, so he checked that. When he couldn't get at it, he ran the directory and tried all the other programs on the disk."

"What happened?"

"Nothing. He was still sitting in front of the

15

computer, muttering 'How strange' when Liz and I left."

"That's strange, all right. Somebody must have erased them," Geoffrey said. "But who? And why?"

"Couldn't it have been some kind of error?" asked Amber's mother. "I'd hate to think of one of your classmates doing anything so malicious. You kids have been working on those projects for months. It must be some kind of mistake."

"No," Geoffrey said. "It isn't easy to erase Abacus programs, and there's no way a whole disk could be wiped out by mistake. That's supposed to be one of the advantages of this system. Also, now I come to think of it, if the programs had been erased, they wouldn't appear on the directory any more."

Amber picked up her fork and pushed a few peas around on her plate.

"Liz and I saw Jonathan coming out of the computer room after school," she said finally. "He got all red in the face and wouldn't even look at us before he took off." Amber paused, then looked up at her parents. "He wasn't supposed to be there."

Everyone was silent while the implications of what Amber had said sunk in. Jonathan was a friend of Geoffrey's. He'd been a fairly regular visitor to the house before his parents' divorce.

"Well, that's crazy," Geoffrey said after a minute. "Jonathan may spend all his time with computers these days, but he'd never do anything like that."

"Then who did? The programs were all there

after lunch when we had our class." Brother and sister glared at each other.

"What's for dessert?" asked Timmy.

"Chocolate pudding," his mother answered absently, her attention on the two older children. "You have to clean your plate first."

Timmy and Tommy exchanged looks of disgust across the table.

"Amber, for all you know, he could have been there for a legitimate reason," suggested Dr. Mitchell.

"I think you and Liz should keep this to yourselves," added Mrs. Mitchell. "It would be terrible if you told everyone you saw Jonathan there, and then it turned out he had nothing to do with it. Besides, Mr. Sharkman may already have discovered what was wrong."

"*Now* can we have dessert?" Timmy and Tommy were getting impatient.

*   *   *

After dinner, as Geoffrey and Amber tackled the dishes, their conversation went back again to the missing programs.

"You didn't say anything to Jaws about Jonathan, did you?" Geoffrey demanded as he poured dish soap liberally into the sink.

"Of course not," Amber snapped. She rummaged in a drawer for a clean towel.

"Geoff," she said, "why don't you ask Jonathan why he was in the computer room?"

"No way," he told her bluntly as he dumped a load of plates into the water. "I'm not sticking my nose into his business. Besides, unless I have something more concrete than the fact that you two pea-brains saw him leave the computer room, I'm going to assume that *if* anything funny is going on, he has nothing to do with it."

"You're probably right," Amber said. She reached for a wet plate. "But just the same, the whole thing seems very strange."

Chapter 3
What's happening?

The rain dripped and plopped through the thick branches of the old maple, straight onto Liz's head. It ran down her forehead and collected on her eyelashes.

"Seven minutes," she muttered, looking at her watch. "Amber is never this late." She shifted her books, leaned back against the rough bark of the tree and impatiently watched the road.

"Sorry," Amber said breathlessly when she arrived a few minutes later. "I just couldn't get going this morning. I kept thinking about *Whodunnit* and wondering what happened."

Liz carefully negotiated a large puddle, then shrewdly eyed her friend. "You mean you can't stop wondering why Jonathan was in the computer room when he wasn't supposed to be, and whether he knows what happened to our program."

Amber pushed a wet strand of hair from her eyes. "Maybe it was an accident."

"Maybe," Liz said slowly.

Amber stopped dead in the middle of the road and glared at her friend. "You don't really suspect Jonathan, do you? He was the one, remember, who helped us program *Whodunnit* in the first place."

"I remember," Liz returned evenly. "But if this gets around the school, everyone will blame him — especially since he's turned into such a loner. We'd better keep that in mind."

"Jonathan couldn't have done it," Amber reassured herself, adjusting a strap on her knapsack. "But what was he doing in there? No one is supposed work on the computers without scheduling it with Jaws."

"I think we'd better find out — somehow," Liz said.

"For sure," Amber agreed. "The sooner, the better."

Liz nodded silently. They had reached the school, and in the crowd of hurrying students, the subject had to be dropped.

Amber pulled open the heavy double doors leading into the busy main hall, then headed for their shared locker, not far from the drinking fountain where students congregated.

"Let's find Jaws first and see if he's solved the problem," Liz suggested as she spun the combination lock. "Maybe we're worried about nothing."

Amber threw her knapsack into the locker and glanced over her shoulder.

"Yes, and fast. Here comes Motormouth. The last thing we need is for her to find out about this mess."

Liz peered down the hall. Sure enough, there was Jane, bearing down on them with four other students from their computer class — Craig

20

Nicholson, Jason Goldstein, Lindsay Watson and Heather Simpson. They looked angry, especially Craig, his brown eyes fixed belligerently on the girls. He liked to come across tough, despite his conservative look.

"I think it's already too late."

"Amber! Liz!" Jane called in her high-pitched, nasal voice.

Amber groaned and hid her head in the locker. "Tell her I have smallpox."

"You mean chicken pox," Liz replied, pulling her friend back out. "Come on, give them your best metal mouth."

Amber smiled, exposing the maximum amount of metal and rubber bands.

"Is it true?" demanded Jane, oblivious as usual. "Is there really a mad hacker at Ash Grove?"

Amber stopped smiling. Liz carefully wiped her nose with a soggy tissue pulled from her coat pocket.

"A what?" Amber demanded tersely.

"You heard me! A mad hacker. Someone wiped out our term projects. We think it was that computer creep."

"What creep?" Liz had a sinking feeling that a riot might be imminent.

"Oh come on, Liz," sneered Jane, hitching up her books.

"Don't act dumber than you are," Craig Nicholson said loudly.

Liz ignored him. He was always trying to be the centre of attention and she wasn't about to help him get what he wanted.

"Everyone knows you saw Jonathan Weiss leave the computer room."

"It's obvious he did it," Jane said. "The projects were okay after lunch."

"Anyone could have done it!" Amber snapped, stepping forward.

"Sure!" Craig said sarcastically. "It's not that easy to erase a series of programs. I should know." He paused for effect. "After all, the Abacus was developed by my dad's company."

"So maybe they aren't erased then," Liz said, forcing a smile. "Maybe Amber and I just pushed a few wrong buttons. What could really go wrong when we have such a knack with computers!"

She leaned dramatically against the locker. Unfortunately, it was still open.

"Like you said, Liz, what could go wrong?" Craig teased when the laughter died down. "Let's go," he said, turning to the others. "With this dynamic duo on the job, why should we worry?"

Still laughing, the rest of the students headed for their lockers. Jane glared at Amber and Liz, then turned on her heel and followed Craig.

"Saved by comic relief," Liz remarked as she struggled out of the locker. She stuffed Amber's gym clothes back into a corner.

"I suppose you're going to tell me you fell into that locker on purpose?"

"You'll never know," Liz replied, grinning. Then her expression sobered. "Who could have told Jane about the missing programs?" she said.

"We know it wasn't us," Amber pointed out.

"And it wasn't Jaws — that's not his style. So how did Jane know they were gone?

"That, my dear Elliot, is the big question."

* * *

Hunched over a book in her first study period, Liz pretended she couldn't hear the angry mutters from her classmates as the news spread.

Jonathan's name floated by with sickening regularity.

Down the hall in the music room, Amber morosely played scales on her oboe. Jane Dobbs was sitting beside her. As inconspicuously as possible, Amber edged her chair towards the door so she could see into the computer room across the hall.

Jaws, his plaid jacket draped over a chair and his sleeves rolled up, was seated in front of an Abacus poring over what looked like his entire collection of programming books. Obviously the problem had not been solved.

Suddenly Amber drew back. The principal, Mr. Cline, was coming down the hall. He headed straight for the computer room, walked in, and started talking to Jaws. Amber couldn't hear what he was saying, but she saw Jaws shake his head in response. So did Jane.

"So much for Jaws to the rescue," she hissed.

Amber drowned her out with her oboe. She saw Jaws pick up his jacket before he and the principal moved out of the terminal room, still discussing the situation.

"As far as I can tell," Jaws was saying, loud enough for Amber to hear every word, "someone has deliberately prevented access to the projects by writing a new program that overrides the other command codes. Until I can break into it, the projects are, in effect, lost."

The principal stopped walking and turned to face Jaws. "Are you sure, Eugene?"

There was a pause. Jaws sighed, adjusted his glasses and looked back at the principal.

"Yes. We're going to have to call the police."

"The police!" Mr. Cline appeared startled. "Isn't that a little drastic for a student prank?"

"We can't treat this as a prank," Jaws said slowly. "Computers are the tools for these children's futures — and the weapons. If we admire the genius of the child who breaks into other systems, we are overlooking the crime. We must call the police."

"Well, Eugene," Mr. Cline said reluctantly, "if you feel that strongly, I'll take the appropriate action."

Jaws nodded and the two men walked down the hall, out of earshot.

"Did you hear that?" demanded Jane. "Now the sparks are really going to fly!"

"I didn't hear anything," Amber growled. "Not a single, blasted, stupid thing." She put her oboe to her lips once again and reeled out the scale — entirely off-key.

*   *   *

By lunch time it was all over the school.

"I can't believe they're going to call the police," Liz said as she and Amber looked over

24

the day's selections in the cafeteria line. She picked up a slice of pizza and sniffed it cautiously.

"You're risking your life with that one," Amber commented. "The crust is toasted foam rubber."

Liz put it back in favour of a second piece of chocolate cream pie. Amber shook her head in disgust.

"Made with milk," Liz explained. "Calcium's great stuff."

They headed to their usual table where some of their friends were already seated.

"Did you hear what's happened now?" Lindsay demanded. "Jaws has called the cops!"

"Jonathan's really in for it now," called Jason from the next table.

"No," Liz exclaimed, "that's not it . . . "

"Hasn't anybody ever heard of 'innocent until proven guilty'?" Amber demanded, her red hair seeming to snap with anger.

"I suppose you're talking about me."

A hush fell over the group. No one had seen Jonathan come in.

He stood in front of them, gripping his lunch tray so hard that his knuckles were painfully white against the black plastic. Liz noticed he was trembling slightly.

"You all think I sabotaged your programs," he said tautly. "I didn't."

"Then what were you doing in the computer room after school yesterday?" challenged Craig.

"That's none of your business," retorted Jonathan. He gave Amber and Liz a shrivelling stare.

"Someone wrote a new program," continued Craig, leaning back in his chair. "Now none of us can retrieve our projects. That would take some pretty fancy programming."

"So?"

"So, you're the genius who's supposed to be able to do anything he wants on the computers, aren't you? You tell me."

"Craig, that's rotten!" Amber exclaimed. "Just because your dad loaned the computers to the school . . . "

"Forget it Amber," Jonathan interrupted, his face flushing red. "He's right. I can do anything I want on the computers. But if I did override those programs, you'd never even figure out that much about how it was done."

"Who else could have done it?" Jane demanded. "You have the brains and you had the opportunity."

"I didn't do it!" Jonathan shouted suddenly, slamming his lunch tray onto the table. The silence was absolute as he raced out the door in a blind fury. Eugene Sharkman, who had cafeteria duty that day, overheard the tail end of the confrontation. He stared thoughtfully at the students, picked up the remains of his bag lunch, and silently slipped out.

"Did you see that look Jonathan gave us?" Liz said in a bewildered voice. "He thinks we told on him!"

Amber scowled at her classmates. They had

gone back to eating their lunches as if nothing had happened.

"What a bunch of . . . of . . . zombies!" she declared. She slammed her own tray down on the table. "Come on Liz," she said furiously, "all of a sudden I've lost my appetite. We're going to find out what's happening around here!"

"I see trouble coming," moaned Liz, giving her uneaten chocolate pie a last, wistful look before depositing it in a nearby garbage bin.

"I don't care," Amber declared militantly. "We have to help Jonathan."

Chapter 4
Police!

The morning bell had already rung when Detective Louis P. Dexter of the Ash Grove Police Force stepped out of the squad car, hitched up his pants, and headed for the school's main door. He was looking forward to paying Ash Grove Junior High a visit.

"Just make it look official," Kenneth Cline had advised him on the telephone the night before. "I want the students to realize this is serious, even if no charges are laid."

"I know just what's needed," Detective Dexter had replied. "I'll bring along a uniformed officer to make it look good."

He had not, however, planned on the eager young rookie at his side. Officer Ernest Jones was a graduate of Ash Grove Junior High, and he was keen to impress the detective with his knowledge of "the scene of the crime."

"This way to the office, sir." He spoke in a low voice because Detective Dexter had explained to him on the way over that — in his experience — it was best to arrive with as little fanfare as possible.

"Unnerves the suspects," the detective said knowingly.

They advanced quietly down the hallway of the school, past rows of anonymous grey lockers.

"Looks like someone was in a hurry," chuckled Detective Dexter softly as he noticed a dirty sweat sock stuck in a locker door. "Some things never change, do they Jones?"

"No sir," replied the rookie, warily eying an advancing female figure. "Some people never change either."

"Why Ernest Jones, is that you?"

"Yes ma'am." Jones whipped off his blue regulation hat and stood at attention. He was painfully aware that the element of surprise was totally lost. Curious faces peered out of several classroom doors. "I'm a police officer now, ma'am."

"So I see," replied Miss Belcher. "And who might this be?" She turned to Detective Dexter with a look of authority perfected over thirty years of teaching.

"Detective Dexter, ma'am. Ash Grove Police Force." He unconsciously straightened, pulling in his sagging stomach.

"You're here to solve this computer crisis, I take it?" asked Miss Belcher, addressing him as though he were one of her less promising pupils.

"Yes ma'am."

"The sooner the better. This is an institution of learning, not a jailhouse. Good day, gentlemen." With that, Miss Belcher dismissed the police, turned, and marched down the hall toward her classroom.

"Who was that?" asked Detective Dexter in awe.

"That was Miss Belcher. My old homeroom teacher. I also had her for French and English — two years in a row!" replied Jones, wincing at the memory.

"We could use her downtown. She'd scare the pants off the criminals," Detective Dexter commented wryly.

*   *

"Detective Dexter. Thanks for coming." Mr. Cline appeared in the doorway of the office. "I hope you didn't leave anything important for our computer prank."

"No problem. This sort of thing has to be nipped in the bud. We don't need another *War Games*, do we?" he chuckled.

"A what?"

"A movie. Some smart aleck kid accidentally breaks into army computers and just about starts World War III. Anyway," he cleared his throat abruptly, "down to business. This is Officer Jones. All we need is a room and a list of people who might shed some light on the problem. We'll take it from there."

"I've got just the spot. Follow me, please." The principal led them around the corner and down two doors to the counselling office.

"It's a bit small, I'm afraid," apologized Mr. Cline. "But you'll have some privacy. There's just a supply room on the other side of the partition."

"Right. This will do fine. Who's the computer science teacher?"

"That's Eugene Sharkman. I've arranged for him to meet you at the end of this period. He'll fill you in. There are several students you should see — and the janitor, Chester Mallory. He's here at odd hours. Maybe he's noticed something unusual."

* * *

Eugene Sharkman shook hands with the detective and then quickly filled him in on the crime.

"You say it must have happened sometime between two and four o'clock in the afternoon?" the detective asked.

"That's right. The students were working on their projects during the period right after lunch. Then when Amber Mitchell and Liz Elliot — they're the two girls who discovered the problem — attempted to retrieve their program after school, nothing happened. I thought at first it was a syntax error on their part or a technical malfunction, but I've ruled those out. Someone overrode the projects with a program preventing access."

"Right . . . uh, right." Detective Dexter nodded his head as though he understood what Mr. Sharkman was talking about. "What about these girls? Could they have done it?"

"Amber and Liz? Impossible. They don't have the knowledge. These Abacus computers are very sophisticated. In fact, we're testing them for Eastern Technology. Robert Nicholson, the vice-president, has a son here at Ash Grove. We're very fortunate to have the use of the computers."

"Why's that?" the detective asked.

"The Abacus is the most advanced personal computer ever made. It's the future — and a wonderful opportunity for our students."

"Hmm . . . that's a coincidence. I was talking to Robert Nicholson, just the other day . . . Anyway, what about this boy, Jonathan Weiss?"

Mr. Sharkman hesitated a moment.

"I don't know. He was there, and there's no doubt he's one of the very few students who could write such a complex program. But he insists he didn't, and I'm inclined to believe him, even though he wouldn't say why he was there. Perhaps he'll tell you."

"I'll see what I can do. What about this janitor, Mallory? Seems he's around a lot."

"He is," Jaws said, "and he always seems to have an answer to everything. But he knows even less about computers than my students."

The call from the office came at the beginning of their biology class:

"Liz Elliot and Amber Mitchell, please report directly to the guidance office."

Amber and Liz looked at each other. Liz swallowed. Jane, their lab partner, smiled nastily.

"Looks like the cops are here."

Amber suddenly beamed and slid a pickled frog over in front of Jane.

"Gee," she said. "What a shame. Looks like you'll have to handle the dissection yourself, Jane."

"Wh-what . . . " Jane stammered.

"Sorry," Amber said. "But we've got things to do."

32

"I'm so nervous, I could die!" blurted Liz as soon as they left the classroom. "All we were doing was minding our own business, and now we're going to be interrogated by the police!"

"I know. I know. But at least we got out of dissecting those frogs. Talk about gross," Amber said, shaking her head. "I wonder about our education system, sometimes."

They walked slowly down the hall.

"What we need is a plan," Amber said as they neared the office.

"What we need," Liz said tartly, "is to find out what Jonathan was doing in the computer room. I suppose he'll have to tell the police."

"That's it!" Amber said.

"What's it?"

"Shh!" Amber grabbed Liz's arm and pulled her back before they could round the corner to the guidance office. "There's a policeman outside the door!"

"So? What are you doing?" Liz hissed, indignantly rubbing her arm.

"I have an idea." Amber whispered the details to Liz, whose face got progressively paler.

"Are you crazy?" she demanded.

"Have you got a better idea?"

"Anything is a better idea," she snapped. "There is no way I'm going to flirt with that policeman. I'm no good at that sort of thing. Besides, I was planning on living to my next birthday. My mother's going to make me a chocolate fudge cake."

33

"Come on, Liz," Amber coaxed. "This is serious. How else am I going to get into the supply room? I'll be able to hear everything from there." She paused as Liz glared at her. "Remember, Jonathan was the one who helped us write our program in the first place. He's our friend."

"Why don't you do it?" Liz moaned.

"Because I wouldn't know where to start. Shy people make the best flirts."

"Is that supposed to be a compliment?"

Amber didn't answer directly. "You will do it, won't you?" she pleaded.

"Why do I let you talk me into these things?" answered Liz. She was still shaking her head when they reached the guidance office.

"And Liz," whispered Amber, just before they reached the door, "don't go back to class without me, okay? Maybe you could wait for me in the washroom so no one will see you. The last thing we need is people asking a whole lot of questions about where I've gone."

Without daring to look at Officer Jones, the girls hurried in.

* * *

Detective Dexter only kept them about ten minutes.

"Close the door on your way out, please."

Carefully Amber pulled the door shut behind them. Jones was standing a short distance away, near the main hall.

"Okay, Liz," breathed Amber. "Do your stuff."

Amber stepped back a few paces toward the

34

supply room door. Liz shot her one last desperate glance, took a deep breath, and approached the policeman.

"Ahem, uh, excuse me officer," she began, her face turning as red as her pullover sweater. "Ah, that's a nice uniform you have on."

Startled, Officer Jones looked down at the buttons gleaming on his chest, blushed, and said, "Uh, thanks. It's regulation . . ."

Silence.

This would not do. She had to get him to turn and face the other way so Amber could sneak into the supply room. She smiled nervously, wiggled a few steps past him, and turned.

"How long have you been a policeman?" she ventured.

"Six months." Jones turned to face her, his back now to Amber. He was glad of the diversion. The morning had been unbelievably boring.

"Do you like it?" asked Liz, fluttering her eyelashes. Being sexy took a lot of ingenuity. Perhaps she could do some research on the subject . . .

"It has its moments. Do you have something in your eye?"

"Uh, no."

Now he was staring at her. "Don't I know you from somewhere?"

"I don't think so." Liz's eyes opened wider. That was the oldest line in the book . . .

"Maybe my kid sister used to baby-sit you or something."

"Yeah, right," replied Liz, thoroughly deflated.

Officer Jones glanced down the hall. "Hey, where'd the other girl go?"

"Oh her? She left a few minutes ago." After all she did go — just not where she was supposed to.

"Well, uh, goodbye . . . It's been really nice talking to you." With a little luck the policeman would not connect Amber's disappearance with her own feeble flirtation.

*   *   *

Amber was uncomfortable. She was squeezed against the supply room's partition, perched on a large box wedged between piles of paper, boxes of chalk, and other endless supplies.

And so far, she hadn't heard a thing.

"Jones!" Detective Dexter called out suddenly. Amber jumped. It sounded as though he was right beside her. She'd be able to hear everything.

The door clicked open.

"Yessir?" Jones answered from the other side of the wall.

"See if you can find that janitor for me. Chester Mallory is his name."

"Mallory? Right away, sir."

The door closed.

Just my luck, thought Amber. I'll have turned to stone by the time Jonathan gets here. And what's Mallory got to do with this anyway?

By the time Jones came back with Mallory, a cramp was knotting Amber's left leg. Miserably she tried to stretch her foot without actually moving. If she could hear the detective, then he could hear her too.

The door in the next room opened abruptly.

"Chester Mallory, sir."

"Thank you, Jones. Mr. Mallory, I'm Detective Dexter. Take a seat, please."

A chair scraped across the floor.

"You've probably heard that we're here to find out who's been tampering with the school computers."

"What's that got to do with me? I don't know anything about it," Mallory protested.

"I didn't say you did," replied Detective Dexter. "But maybe you've noticed some unusual activity around the computer room? Anyone there who shouldn't have been?"

"Anyone who shouldn't have been there?" Mallory began cautiously. "There's that Weiss kid, and those two nosey girls — a redhead with a smart mouth and a brunette. They were hanging around after school the other day. They're probably up to something with Weiss," he added. "They're always in trouble around here. I'd know if there was anyone else."

On the other side of the partition, Amber was burning. What did Mallory think he was doing anyway? She'd show him who had a smart mouth! The nerve! Furious, she swept her hair back with her hand. She didn't notice the chalk on the shelf by her elbow.

The box crashed loudly to the floor. Shattered pieces flew in all directions.

Her career as a detective was finished!

Chapter 5
Undercover

"What was that?" Detective Dexter's voice rang sharply from the other side of the partition.

Amber held her breath and shut her eyes. Don't move . . .

"Oh that's just someone in the supply room next door," the janitor said. "Teachers send the students in there all the time to get stuff. Some dumb kid probably dropped a box of pencils or something."

"I see. In that case, where were we?"

Amber couldn't quite believe her good luck. She opened her eyes cautiously. No capture. No long march to the principal — in handcuffs.

"So, Amber Mitchell, Liz Elliot, and Jonathan Weiss were the only students you saw near the computer room outside regular class hours yesterday?"

"That's what I said," replied Mallory. "Hey, look, can I go now? I've got a lot of work to do around this place."

"Yes. That's all for now," the detective said. "If you remember anything else, call me."

"Yeah, sure."

A chair rasped across the floor. The door opened, then closed loudly.

Good, thought Amber. He's leaving. Now we can get on to the important part — Jonathan.

She waited. Another chair scraped. Swish, creak — window shades were being adjusted. Footsteps. The chair scraped again. Papers rustled. Silence.

Come on, urged Amber inside her head. Keeping a cautious eye on the chalk, she moved a leg that was going numb.

She counted packages of paper and stacks of notebooks on the shelf beside her. She'd never realized how much stuff was needed to keep Ash Grove Junior High in business. Where was Jonathan? What was taking him so long?

The bell rang for lunch. Amber's stomach gurgled right on schedule. Longingly, she thought of the peanut butter sandwich, apple, and chocolate chip cookies in her knapsack. The way things were going, she would starve to death before Jonathan even showed up.

*   *   *

Moodily, Liz stuffed the wrapper from her sandwich into the waste receptacle.

"Some plan this is," she grumbled to her reflection in the mirror. "Amber's undercover and I'm hiding in the washroom, eating lunch. Nancy Drew never had to do this!"

Impatiently she paced the floor.

"Amber, how can you do this to me? And what am I supposed to say if she doesn't show up

39

for the next class? I don't want to spend my life in the detention room!"

She stopped in front of the mirror again, tried to smooth her hair, and remembering her encounter with Officer Jones, experimented briefly with an enticing smile.

"Ugh! Amber where are you? I can't take much more of this!"

She was so busy talking to herself, she almost missed the sound of the outer door opening. Someone was coming in! Frantically, she looked around, then dashed into a cubicle. Wouldn't you know it, the only one with a missing toilet seat lid. And no lock on the door! She thought for a moment of sitting down anyway. Then she remembered her socks. They were a bright red and green plaid. If anyone should happen to look under the door and see them, they would know for sure who was in there.

She leapt up on the toilet seat and crouched down, praying for balance and Amber's speedy return.

"If you ask me," Jane Dobbs was saying in her unmistakable whine, "Amber's hot for Jonathan. Why else would she stick up for him?"

"Amber always sticks up for people," replied the other girl. "She's been doing it since kindergarten."

That has to be Karen Lee, Liz thought.

"But why Jonathan?" insisted Jane, raising her voice so she could be heard over the water running in the sink. "The guy's got a computer for a brain and not much else."

"So, he's shy. I think he's nice. Besides, maybe he's innocent. Did that ever occur to you?"

Liz cheered silently from her perch. Not everyone was out to blame Jonathan after all.

"He had to have done it. Who else could have? And I want to know where Amber and Liz are. They've been gone an awfully long time. The police wouldn't have sent for Jonathan if they were still talking to those two. They didn't even show up for lunch. They're up to something."

"Probably," replied Karen. "They usually are. But I'll bet they won't tell you."

"Come on, let's go," said Jane.

"Just a minute, I've got to go to the washroom."

Liz lost her balance and almost fell in the toilet.

Then the door swung open and there she was, perched on the facilities like a vulture with cramps.

The colour drained from Karen's face.

Liz grabbed some toilet paper and shoved it at her.

Karen stared back at her. "I think I'll go later," she called to Jane.

"What's the matter?" Jane asked. "Toilet backed up again? This school is so gross."

"You can say that again." Karen grinned at Liz and shut the door.

* * *

Amber's ears perked up. The door to the guidance room had opened. Finally, some action.

"Come in, son," Detective Dexter called.

41

"You wanted to see me, sir?"

"Take a seat, Jonathan. I've got a few questions for you. I'm Detective Dexter."

Poor Jonathan, thought Amber. He must be scared to death.

There was a pause. Amber could hear papers being shuffled again.

"You know about the problem with the computer, Jonathan?"

"Yes . . . yes, sir."

"Apparently you were in the computer room just before the problem was discovered."

Jonathan did not reply.

"Mr. Sharkman tells me he keeps a careful record of the students who use the computer. Is that right?"

"Yes, sir. It's part of the testing we're doing for Eastern Technology," Jonathan explained.

"But your name isn't in the logbook for that day."

The detective paused. Amber leaned forward.

"No, sir," Jonathan said quietly.

"Then why were you in the computer room?"

Amber waited, not daring to breath. Finally!

The supply room door banged open.

"I'll just be a minute. My teacher needs some paper," a voice called.

Amber froze, then slowly turned. Craig Nicholson! Frantically, she signalled him to be quiet.

Eyebrows raised, and a quizzical smile on his face, he mouthed the words, "What are you doing here?"

"Who me?" she whispered in a strained voice.

"No, the invisible man."

"Shhh . . . they'll hear you."

"Why, you little sneak," Craig whispered back as the truth hit him. "You're eavesdropping!"

"Quiet!" Amber mouthed.

Jonathan was talking. "I had a good reason to be there. It had nothing to do with those programs."

"That's not good enough, son. You'll have to tell me exactly why you were there," replied Detective Dexter firmly.

"And if I don't?" asked Jonathan quietly.

"Then I'll have to assume you're guilty."

There was no reply.

"Craig, stay still," hissed Amber. "I can't hear with you squirming around."

"Son," tried the detective again, using a softer tone, "just tell me what you were doing in the computer room. It will be better for everyone."

"I was testing a program of my own," Jonathan said finally.

"But why didn't you clear it with Mr. Sharkman? I don't understand."

"We aren't allowed to use the Abacus computers for anything but school work. This is for a contest. Eastern Technology is giving away a thousand dollars and a scholarship for the best video game. The Abacus has new capabilities that I was trying to use. I thought they'd give me a better chance at winning. But I had to test run it. I'm . . . I'm sorry."

Amber suspected Jonathan was close to tears.

"All right, son. I believe you're telling the truth, but I'll need to see the disk you've got that game on. Go on back to your class now."

Amber glanced at Craig. His face was as white as the paper he had come to the supply room to get.

"I didn't know about that," he pleaded in a whisper. "I forgot all about that contest at ET . . . I should never have listened to Jane. How could I have been so stupid . . . " he trailed off miserably.

Amber looked at him curiously, but her attention was drawn back to the guidance room before the importance of what he had said sunk in.

"Jones, come in here please."

"Sir?"

"Was there anyone in the supply room while I was talking to the janitor?"

"No, sir," the officer replied. "There's a kid in there now, though. He's taking his time, too."

"Better check that out," the detective said crisply.

Craig and Amber looked at each other.

"I'm dead!" Amber whispered.

"We're both dead!"

"Quick!" Amber hissed. "Behind the door!"

They slid in behind the door just as the policeman entered the room. He took a quick look around, turned out the light, and shut the door.

"Don't move," whispered Amber. "We're liable to crash into something in the dark."

"I'm not going anywhere," came the anguished reply. "My legs are like jelly."

"Looks like we're stuck until they leave."

* * *

"There's no one there now, sir," reported Jones. "He must have left when you called me in here."

"Hmm . . . all right," Detective Dexter said slowly. "That janitor was awfully quick to point the finger at those three kids. No good reason that I could see, either."

"Sir?"

Dexter leaned back in his chair and studied the ceiling.

"Last week Robert Nicholson called me about a security problem at Eastern Technology. There's big money involved, Nicholson told me. Very big money."

"Jones," he said, sitting up abruptly. "I think we should have another chat with the principal . . ."

Chapter 6
Whodunnit?

The door to the guidance room slammed shut.

"They've gone!" breathed Amber. "We've got to get out of here before anyone sees us." She groped for the door handle. "Craig? Are you still here?"

"What? Oh, Amber . . . yeah, let's go." Craig's voice quivered in the darkness.

He's sure isn't as tough as he pretends to be, Amber thought smugly. From the tone of his voice, you'd think he'd been caught in the act.

Cautiously, she opened the door and peered down the corridor, blinking as her eyes adjusted to the light.

"The coast is clear."

They slipped into the hall. Craig eased the door shut.

"We'd better move," Amber urged, checking her watch. "There's only five minutes left in this period and I still haven't eaten any lunch."

When Craig just stood there, Amber looked at him quizzically.

"Amber," he began, fingering the edges of the paper, "do you think Jonathan is in bad trouble for using the Abacus?"

"What? With Liz and me on the job? We're

already halfway to clearing him, not to mention getting to the bottom of this whole mess," Amber replied, high on the success of her first venture as a private eye. "The real tough part, though, is going to be finding out just who did write that program."

But Craig wasn't listening. He just muttered, "See you later," and started to walk away.

"Hey! Wait a minute." Amber hurried to catch up. "Thanks for keeping quiet. I could have gotten into trouble in a big way there."

Craig said nothing. Lost in his own thoughts, he continued on down the hall, leaving Amber standing indignantly, hands on hips, a puzzled scowl on her face.

"It's catching," she said to the empty hall-way. "Everyone at Ash Grove is acting weird. First Jonathan. Now Craig. Who's next?"

"Psst! Amber!" Liz whispered loudly from the washroom down the hall. "Come on! The bell's going to ring!" She was clutching Amber's books and waving her lunch bag.

Forget Craig, Amber thought. Her stomach became her number one priority. She sprinted down the hall and snatched her lunch.

"I'm starved."

"Quick! Back in the washroom," urged Liz.

"Hey, where are my cookies?" Amber demanded as she rummaged through her lunch bag on the counter above the sinks.

"I was nervous," answered Liz. "You know I have to eat when I'm nervous. Besides, it was a long wait. A very long wait, Amber. What happened? I thought you'd been caught and shipped off to Alcatraz."

"Very funny," Amber replied, biting into her sandwich. "They'd never catch me," she boasted through a mouthful of peanut butter and jam. "Anyway, Alcatraz was closed years ago."

"Must have heard you were coming."

"Ha, ha . . . Just wait until I tell you what I heard. We were right. Jonathan didn't do it!"

"Great! I knew it."

"And," said Amber between bites, "I also heard an interesting conversation between Detective Dexter and dear Mr. Mallory. Do you know what that lying, no good, repulsive degenerate said about us — two of the nicest, most upstanding girls you could ever meet?"

"Save it for the dragon lady," Liz said impatiently. "What did you hear?"

Amber swallowed and opened her mouth to comply just as the bell rang, ending the lunch period. "No time now. We have to hurry. I'll tell you on the way to French."

"You'd better." They joined the stream of students changing classes. "And I have something to tell you, too. I did a little undercover work of my own."

"Oh?"

"I was keeping a low profile like you told me, and guess who came in to use the facilites?"

Amber grimaced.

"Let me guess — the one, the only, Miss Jane Dobbs."

"You got it."

"She keeps turning up," mused Amber. "Come to think of it, so does Craig. And he's acting real weird. I wonder what's really going on here . . ."

48

                              *   *   *

"My house?" Liz asked as Amber spun the combination on their locker at the end of the day.

"Do you have twin brothers?"

"Definitely my house," Liz agreed. "Providing that sometime today you get around to
telling me everything Jonathan told the police. If
I don't find out soon, I'm going to explode with
curiosity."

"And so will I!" called a loud voice. Jane
appeared out of the crowd of hurrying students. "I
know you two are up to something, and I intend
to find out what it is. Isn't it lucky we all live
near each other? I can walk home with you!"

                              *   *   *

Fifteen minutes later, the girls left a disgruntled
Jane at the corner of Maple and Broadview.

"I'd say we handled Jane rather well,
wouldn't you, Liz?" asked Amber, switching off
her portable radio.

"What do you mean *we*? The minute we left
school, you put on your earphones and tuned her
out. I handled her!"

"Well done, partner," Amber said, patting
Liz on the back. "That's what friends are for,
after all."

"Amber!" Liz screeched. Amber laughed and
raced ahead, up the stone walk to the Elliot
house.

The old two-storey frame structure was
flanked by high maples. They'd been planted so
long ago, no one could remember whether the
trees or the house came first.

The front door opened as Amber reached it.

"So, you girls are here. Good. Good!" Olga, the Elliot's long-time housekeeper, gave both girls a hug.

"Are Mom and Dad home?" asked Liz, dropping her knapsack on the bench in the vestibule.

"No. Your mother had to call a special City Council meeting and won't be home until late, and your papa just telephoned from his office at the university. He has to meet with the Graduate Student Committee or some such thing, but he will be here for dinner."

"Great. I was afraid they'd be having people for cocktails or something," said Liz. "Amber and I have a lot of work to do. But can we please have a snack? Lunch was a little hectic today."

"It sure smells good in here," Amber added, looking hopeful.

Olga laughed. "I made cookies this afternoon."

They followed her into the kitchen. Amber called home while Liz piled cookies on a plate and Olga poured milk.

"I'm glad Dad's going to be home for dinner," she confided to the housekeeper. "Mom and I have this great idea for our summer vacation . . ."

The housekeeper shook her head goodnaturedly. "You and your mother have that man wrapped around your little fingers!" She handed each girl a glass of milk. "No crumbs, you two — I just vacuumed!"

But the girls were already on their way up to Liz's bedroom.

"Finally," said Liz. She leaned against her

headboard with a glass of milk in one hand and a cookie in the other. "Now tell me everything."

"In a minute," said Amber, taking another cookie from the plate. She made herself comfortable in the rocking chair by the window and put her feet up on the sill.

"You know," she said slowly, "at first I was really excited by what I heard today, but the more I think about it, the more I realize I didn't really hear anything."

"Amber, you are dangerously straining a long-standing friendship."

Amber grinned, revealing a mouth full of braces and cookie crumbs.

"I'll tell you what I mean. First I heard Mallory — that reject from a robot factory — try to pin the blame on us. And then I heard Jonathan say he was innocent. According to what he told the police, he'd been in the computer room testing a program of his own for an Eastern Technology contest."

"What contest?"

"ET is giving away prizes for the best new video game. Jonathan was going to enter it. College scholarship or something."

"Guess he'll need it, since his dad split," Liz said thoughtfully. "So he just happened to be in the wrong place at the wrong time."

"That's right. But it still doesn't tell us who messed up our class project. That's what I meant when I said I really didn't hear anything."

Amber lurched out of the chair and paced restlessly around the room. She took another cookie then went back to the window and stared out, chewing thoughtfully.

"There has to be a clue somewhere, but we just haven't recognized it," said Amber, turning to face Liz. "At least, that's the way it works in good detective stories."

"Motive and opportunity," replied Liz from her position on the bed.

"What?"

"Motive and opportunity. The person who did it had to have a reason for doing it — unlike Aunt Agatha. And he or she" — Liz paused significantly — "had to have had a chance to do it. It's not that easy to get into the computer room. Remember, Jaws locks it before he goes home. But if Jonathan could get in that afternoon, so could somebody else."

"That's right. And," said Amber, eagerly grasping Liz's train of thought, "it also had to be someone who knows enough about computers to write a program that would override all the others stored on that disk."

"That lets us out," commented Liz.

"No kidding," agreed Amber. "But don't you see? That's everyone was so quick to believe that Jonathan did it. Besides being such a loner, he's the only one in school who could write a program difficult enough to stump Jaws."

"How do we know that?"

"What?"

"How do we know for sure he's the only one who knows how to do that? Jaws could probably do it."

"Liz! Get serious!"

Liz twirled a strand of hair around her finger.

"I know Jaws didn't do it," she said earnestly, "but the point is that we don't *know* how hard it would be. It could have been anyone who knows more about programming than we do. There are a lot of hackers around — maybe even Mallory."

"Him? No chance."

"I know! It's Miss Belcher! She's the mad hacker of Ash Grove!"

"Liz!"

"I can see it all now. Miss Belcher diverts suspicion by framing two innocent students — us. Then . . ."

"Donning her sneakers," Amber interjected gleefully, "size twenty-four — she creeps, step by step, up to the computer room, and confronts her rival!"

"The Abacus!" shouted Liz. "The other woman in Eugene's life!"

"Oh stop!" begged Amber, clutching her stomach. "I'll be sick all over your room!"

"You'd better not be," replied Liz, clearing her throat in an effort to regain her composure. "Now, back to work."

"Right," agreed Amber, wiping her eyes. "We have to be logical. You're sure it's not Miss Belcher?"

"*Amber!*"

"Okay . . . okay! I just had this awesome image of her in handcuffs being led away by Detective Dexter . . . All right. Logical. This is exactly what happened when I was in the supply room." Carefully she related her adventures to Liz, this time in more detail. "Other than Jonathan, there are two names that do keep popping up — Craig's and Jane's."

"Let's write everything down," suggested Liz, "and then compare notes."

It was almost dinnertime before they had finished charting the whereabouts of everyone they could think of — teachers, friends, even Mallory — on the afternoon the programs were lost.

"Great," Liz said in exasperation as they surveyed their work. "We've established that no one could have done it. Everyone was where they were supposed to be the whole time. Except us of course. Maybe we did it. We weren't in the gym for the first ten minutes, but everyone else was."

"That's it!" exclaimed Amber suddenly. "That's the missing piece of the puzzle. Everyone else was *not* in the gym! Don't you remember?" She grabbed Liz in excitement. "Jane gave us the clue! She told us when we came in late that Craig Nicholson had gone to see the nurse on some phony excuse!"

"That's right! And," added Liz in growing excitement, "he's bound to know a lot about computers, especially the Abacus. His dad's section at ET is the one that's developing and promoting them."

"It was Craig," Amber said triumphantly. "It must have been Craig!"

Chapter 7
Guilty or not guilty?

"All right, class, settle down." Mr. Sharkman raised his voice over the din.

"Open your books to today's assignment, please. Yes, Liz? What is it?"

Liz stood up beside her desk. She looked terrible. Her hair hung in her face, her eyelids drooped, her shoulders sagged. Even her hands were shaking.

Pathetic, Amber thought, grinning behind her textbook.

"I don't feel too well, Mr. Sharkman," Liz said in a faint voice. "May I please be excused?"

"Of course," he answered, peering at her over his glasses. "You do look a touch off-colour, Liz. Do you want someone to take you to the nurse's office?"

"No, no. I'll be fine. If I could just lie down for a while . . . "

Trying not to rush, she collected her books and left the room.

She had to admit, Amber had been right. Her nervous stomach made her the perfect candidate for the job. In fact, she now had every intention of either lying down or throwing up, once she got to the nurse's office. After all, it was part of the plan . . .

"If Craig is the mad hacker of Ash Grove," Amber had reasoned, "he must have pretended to be sick that day so he could get out of gym class to sabotage our programs."

"That was Jaws' free period," Liz had agreed slowly, "so he knew there would be no class in the computer room. But how are we supposed to prove that he did it?"

"We'll have to get a look at the nurse's record book in her office. If Craig really was sick, the time in and out will be written in that book."

"And we'll know whether or not he's guilty."

"Right."

"There's just one small problem," Liz pointed out. "There is no way Mrs. Ramiro is going to let us browse through her records."

"That's where you come in, partner . . . "

*   *   *

The door to the nurse's office was wide open. Hesitantly, Liz entered the room. It was one thing getting past Jaws with a fake sick act; getting past the school nurse was not going to be quite so easy.

"Mrs. Ramiro?" Liz called in a thin, wobbly voice. "Are you there?"

"Yes, I am. Come through to the back room."

There was no turning back now. Nervously, Liz scanned the office, looking for the record book. It was right where Amber had said it would be, on Mrs. Ramiro's desk. The trick would be getting a look at it.

Liz entered the examining room, clutching her books against her chest and swallowing repeatedly.

"Hello, Mrs. Ramiro."

"Well, hello, Liz Elliot," answered the nurse, turning from the cabinet where she had been straightening medical supplies. "I haven't seen you for a while. Not feeling well today?"

Liz smiled feebly and shrugged. "I've got a headache, and my stomach feels a little funny." That's true enough, she thought. A tension headache and a nervous stomach.

Mrs. Ramiro pointed to the cot against the wall. "You just lie down over there, and I'll take your temperature. I hope we're not starting another flu epidemic. Having to look after you kids puts entirely too much weight on these tired, old feet of mine." She smiled cheerfully.

Liz dutifully laid her books on the cabinet and lay back on the cot while the nurse popped a thermometer in her mouth and covered her with a blanket.

"Craig Nicholson wasn't feeling well the other day. Did he have the flu?" garbled Liz.

"I can't understand a word you're saying with that thing in your mouth," replied Mrs. Ramiro. "Stop talking or you'll break my thermometer."

Liz lay back, exasperated. Getting the information casually from Mrs. Ramiro was not going to work. She'd have to rely on Plan A — inspecting the book.

The nurse interrupted her thoughts. "It was about 9:20 when you came in, wasn't it, Liz?"

"Mmpff."

"I'll go enter it in my book." She disappeared from the room. Less than a minute later, she bustled back and removed the thermometer from Liz's mouth.

"Normal," she pronounced.

Rats, thought Liz.

"But you just stay here and relax for a while. You can go back to class when you're feeling better."

Liz gave it another shot. "Mrs. Ramiro, did Craig—"

Mrs. Ramiro eyed her patient sternly. "Not another word. Close your eyes. That's an order." And once again she left the room.

So much for subtlety, thought Liz. She would just have to lie here and wait for an opportunity to examine Mrs. Ramiro's records. In the meantime, she might as well close her eyes for a minute or two. She'd lain awake late last night planning today's strategy. She really was awfully sleepy . . .

*   *   *

The bell echoed shrilly throughout the school. Liz woke up with a jerk.

"Oh no!" she cried, peering closely at her watch. "Some detective I turned out to be. Talk about lying down on the job!"

Resolutely, she sat up. There was no noise coming from the other room. She grabbed her books and tiptoed to the doorway. Cautiously, she looked around. Empty.

Heart thumping, Liz crossed through the

office and stuck her head out the hall door. No one in sight but Chester Mallory, mopping the floor at the far end of the corridor. Apparently the students had already settled into their next classes.

Liz turned and made a beeline for the desk. The record book was still there, lying open at the day's date. There was a note on top of it.

Dear Liz: If you're feeling better after your nap, enter the time beside your name in the book and return to class. If not, lie back down and wait for me. I've just gone to the office for a few minutes.
Mrs. Ramiro.

What a break, thought Liz. Quickly she flipped through the book to the date of the computer disaster. A girl in eighth grade had twisted her ankle, but that was all. No Craig!

Gleefully, Liz turned the pages back and wrote the time beside her name. Her mission accomplished, she grabbed her belongings and left.

"The dynamic duo triumphs again!" she announced for her own benefit.

The janitor stopped mopping to watch Liz cavort down the hall. His normally sullen face twisted into an even more pronounced scowl.

* * *

"But why? That's the part I don't understand," Liz said earnestly, leaning across the lunch table so no one else could hear her.

"Oh, fishsticks!" replied Amber, vigorously crumpling her sandwich wrapper. "I don't want to turn Craig over to the police. He's a loudmouth but he's okay. Why couldn't it have been Mallory or somebody we can't stand? Why couldn't it have been Jane?"

"So what do we do now?" asked Liz, absently playing with her milk carton. "It doesn't seem right to just go and tell Jaws."

"You're right," Amber agreed. "Besides, yesterday in the supply room, he didn't rat on me, so I'm not telling on him. At least not until we hear his side of the story."

"He's almost finished his lunch," Liz said, looking over to the table where Craig had been eating with his friends.

"All right partner," Amber said. "Let's head him off."

They gathered the remnants of their lunches, deposited the garbage in the trash, and waited just outside the door for Craig. He pushed his way through it a moment later.

"Hey Craig," Amber said, stepping in front of him. "Liz and I want to talk to you for a minute."

"What about?" His voice was tight.

"I think we should go somewhere more private," interjected Liz. "There are too many people around with big ears. And Miss Belcher's on cafeteria duty."

"You don't want the whole school to know what we've got to talk to you about," Amber added. "Look what rumours did to Jonathan."

Craig scowled, but followed them past the cafeteria to the short passageway between the gym and the janitor's office. Mallory's door was shut. The gym was silent and empty. Craig folded his arms across his chest, leaned against the wall, and waited. Amber went right to the point.

"We know you did it, Craig."

"Did what?"

"Cut it out," Liz said. "I checked Mrs. Ramiro's record book. You weren't anywhere near the nurse's office on Monday. You were in the computer room."

Craig studied a row of yellow bricks on the wall above Amber's head.

"So what? Maybe I had a program to run."

"You don't have to sneak time on a school computer," Liz told him. "Your house must be full of computers."

Craig turned to her angrily. "Yeah, sure! That's what you think! There isn't even one computer at my house. My father works with them all day, so he doesn't want to have any around when he comes home. He was a hacker when nobody was, but he's decided I need to be more well-rounded — play sports, have friends. 'Don't bury yourself in bits and bytes,' he says . . . " Craig broke off.

Amber and Liz looked at each other helplessly.

"If it weren't for your stupid Aunt Agatha, nobody would have known about the security lock until Friday afternoon," Craig went on. "I figured that when Jaws tried to load the projects during class, I'd let him puzzle about it for a few minutes, then I'd show him how I did it. I just wanted him to see what a good programmer I can be."

"So you didn't erase our projects?" interrupted Amber.

"No, I blocked access to them with another program. That's why they're still listed on the directory."

"But you let Jonathan take the blame when all he was doing was testing his program for the ET contest."

"At least *he* gets to enter it."

"What do you mean?" asked Liz.

"Dad works at ET, so I'm disqualified. Besides, he'd never even think I might be interested. I just don't get it. He never helps me with my computer projects. He doesn't even know I'm any good. And I *am* good. Even Jaws doesn't know it. Somebody else — like Jonathan — is always the whiz kid."

"Oh."

Craig sighed and looked at the floor.

"I feel really bad about this," he said after a minute. "I didn't think Jonathan would get more than a razzing. I know I shouldn't have gone along with Jane, but Mallory'd already told her you saw Jonathan coming out of the computer room, and I guess I was sick of Jaws always thinking Jonathan's so great. How was I supposed to know Cline would go running to the police? The whole thing got out of hand." He looked pleadingly at Liz and Amber.

"So Jonathan was in the wrong place at the wrong time," said Amber slowly. "We spotted him there, and Jane spread the news."

"That's right," Craig said.

"The way I see it," Liz said, "it took all of us to screw things up, so now I think it's up to all of us to fix them."

"How are we supposed to do that?" demanded Craig. "Everyone knows now that Jonathan didn't do it. Maybe if we don't say anything, it'll all blow over," he added lamely.

"Except for one thing," Liz pointed out. "Jaws still hasn't retrieved our programs. You'll have to tell him sooner or later."

Craig took a minute to digest this.

"There's . . . uh . . . there's one more problem . . ."

"What else did you do, Craig?" demanded Liz suspiciously.

"The Belcher curve."

"The what?"

"The Belcher curve. I came across our English tests on another disk when I was fooling around with the Abacus. I . . . uh, adjusted them slightly."

"You did?" Amber smiled suddenly. English was not her best subject. "*Up*, I hope?"

"Amber!" Liz turned to Craig. "You might have been able to work it out with Jaws. But Miss Belcher? Forget it. She'll get you kicked out of school."

Craig slumped against the wall.

"I'm finished, then. My dad will kill me."

"If there's anything left when the dragon lady's through with you."

"Great, Liz. Thanks a lot . . ."

"Hold on. Maybe it's not too late," interrupted Amber. Her eyes sparkled as she envisioned yet another mission for the dynamic duo. "Maybe, just maybe, we can get into the computer room and readjust the marks and erase the security program."

"I suppose it's worth a try," agreed Liz cautiously. "Providing we don't get caught. That would make Mallory's accusations seem right on."

"I'd do anything at this point," Craig admitted, "even risk getting caught in the computer room, if we could just get all this straightened out."

"Okay, we'll meet back here after the last bell," instructed Amber. "The computer room should be empty."

* * *

The room was empty, but it was locked.

"Rats," Amber declared. "Liz, you read everything. Know anything about break and entry?"

"Sorry," Liz said. "I hadn't anticipated becoming a career criminal."

They stared at the lock, then at each other.

"Now what am I going to do?" sighed Craig as they turned to go.

"You'll have to confess," said Liz, hiking up her books. "Better do it before Miss Belcher discovers what you've done though. She told us we'd get the tests back before the end of the week. This is Thursday."

"It's too bad we couldn't fix the Belcher curve," said Amber, "but I can't wait to see her face when she gets those marks — especially mine. Not that I want you to get into any more trouble than you have to," she added for Craig's benefit.

"Yeah," Craig said glumly. He paused on the steps to zip up his windbreaker, then shoved his hands into his pockets.

"I guess I'll see you tomorrow."

"Yeah, bye, Craig."

"See you, Craig."

Craig walked home slowly. Over and over, he tried to figure out what to do about the mess he was in.

"How could I have been so stupid," he said aloud as he turned up the long, curved driveway to the Nicholson place. The big picture window stared blankly out at him, making the house look awfully empty, he thought as he pulled out his key. He wished his mom was waiting behind the door to greet him, but she'd told him she'd be playing squash that night. Usually, he didn't mind being home alone.

He dropped his books on the velvet chair in the hall, thought better of it, and took them upstairs to his bedroom. The only sound in the whole house was his own breathing.

Back downstairs in the kitchen, he opened a can of pop and sat down. If he didn't get back into that computer room, he was dead. Now he realized how Jonathan must have felt all week.

If only there were someone he could talk to. On impulse, he picked up the telephone and dialed his father's number.

"Mr. Nicholson's office," said the receptionist.

"I'd like to speak to him, please," Craig asked nervously. "It's his son."

"Oh, Craig." The receptionist hesitated. "Your father's in conference and he told me he's not to be disturbed."

"It's kind of important," Craig tried again.

"Is it an emergency? I really can't put you through to him otherwise."

"No . . . no . . . I guess not. Thanks, anyway." He hung up the phone. "Just life and death . . . "

*   *   *

Amber and Liz were almost home.

"Amber," Liz said thoughtfully, "did you catch what Craig said about Mallory this afternoon?"

"You mean that bit about telling Jane we saw Jonathan in the computer room?"

"Yes, and just how did he know that? What's he trying to pull? He's a grouch, but why try and make trouble for us? It doesn't make sense," mused Liz.

"He's just a nerd," said Amber, dismissing the problem. "Our first job is to fix the Belcher curve."

"So, how do we do that, Madame Detective?"

"How, my trusty companion? We go by dark of night!"

Chapter 8
By dark of night!

At precisely seven o'clock, Liz arrived at their rendezvous under the maple tree. She checked her watch, looked up, then stared in disbelief.

"Amber! Not the twins . . . what's going on?" demanded Liz when Amber, two small brothers in tow, reached the tree. "We weren't really supposed to be going to the library! It was only our cover story."

"Hi, Dizzy Lizzy," said Tommy.

"Don't call me that, brat!"

"I couldn't help this," explained Amber crossly, struggling with a book on dinosaurs which was threatening to escape from the pile under her arm. "When I said I was going to the library with you, Dad asked if I could return a book for him, then Geoffrey asked if I could return one for him, and then the twins just happened to have about ten books due tomorrow, and Mom said I should take them and make sure I get back by 8:15. What could I say?"

Liz groaned.

"All right, all right. We'll just have to make the best of it. Here give me some of those." She relieved Amber of half the books.

"You're just mad because we came and Geoffrey didn't," said Timmy, eyes alight with mischief.

"Yes," added Tommy. He started to chant, "Lizzy loves Geoffrey! Lizzy loves Geoffrey!" Not to be outdone by his brother, Timmy joined in. The two boys scampered ahead, out of Liz's reach.

"I'll get you, you little monsters!" she screeched, racing off down the sidewalk after them, leaving Amber giggling behind.

After about a block, Liz gave up the chase and sheepishly waited for her friend. The twins stopped, too, but wisely stayed out of reach.

"I know, I know," said Liz when Amber caught up. "I should just ignore them."

"At least you don't have to live with them."

They fell into step and discussed their next move.

"We can't just leave the twins at the library while we go back to school," Liz said.

"Why not?" asked Amber. "My mom does. She leaves them at the library for story hour all the time. Besides, it should only take a few minutes to get over to the school and fix the Belcher curve. There's an Adult Ed. course in programming at the school tonight, and I'm betting that they leave the computer room door open while it's on, so the students can work on the computers after class."

"You're sure you know how to fix the Belcher curve?"

"No problem," Amber assured her. "I called Craig to get the details before I left."

"Did he guess what we're planning?"

"No, he just thought I was curious about how he programmed the curve. I guess he's been

68

bursting to talk to someone about it, and had no one he could tell."

Liz shook her head. "I sure hope we can fix this. Craig is in enough trouble without Miss Belcher on his case. If we can readjust the grades tonight, she'll never know."

"And what Miss Belcher doesn't know, won't hurt her."

"You mean us," observed Liz drily.

They raced up the steps of the Ash Grove Public Library and entered the hushed, cool interior. After they dropped the books off at the return counter, they went in search of the twins, who'd arrived ahead of them. They found them in the children's section, sitting on the floor, poking around in a shelf of picture books.

"Come and help us," they chorused when they saw the girls.

"Sure," said Amber. She and Liz got down on their knees on the carpeted floor and began to sort through the books. It took about twenty minutes to satisfy both Timmy and Tommy — everything was either *yucko* or they had already read it.

"Now, I want you to take your books and sit over there, and read them," instructed Amber, pointing to the table and chairs by the card catalogues. "You can do some of the puzzles there too, if you want. Liz and I have to go over to the school for a few minutes to, uh . . . to get a book from my locker. Don't move," she added, shaking her finger for emphasis.

"We won't," the boys assured her. They carried their stacks of books to the table and settled down contentedly.

"Why is it I don't trust them?" asked Liz under her breath as they made for the exit.

"Because you know what they're like. Which is why I took the extra precaution of bribing them. We have to take them out for ice cream on Saturday. Chocolate."

"Good thinking," said Liz. "All we need is for them to get into trouble now."

"No kidding."

Once outside the library, they headed rapidly for the school, six blocks away.

"I sure hope we can get into the building after all this," worried Liz.

"No problem. I'm sure there's night school tonight — the building has to be open. We'll just slip in, use the Abacus for a few minutes, and slip out again. No one will even know we've been there."

"I hope you're right," Liz said as they turned the last corner. "We could get into a lot of trouble for this. And I don't think my parents could cope with a problem child . . . "

Her concerns fell on deaf ears. Amber was striding ahead with all the confidence in the world.

"What did I tell you?" Amber pointed triumphantly as they passed the parking lot adjacent to the school. "Look at all those cars. Ash Grove Junior High is open for business. And if Ash Grove Junior High is open for business, chances are the computer room will be, too."

Her eyes were shining in anticipation, Liz noted with disgust. Didn't Amber ever get butterflies?

"We'll synchronize our watches," Amber

declared, coming to an abrupt stop in the middle of the sidewalk. "What time have you got?"

Despite herself, Liz began to get caught up in her friend's enthusiasm.

"Okay. I've got exactly 7:36. It shouldn't take more than fifteen minutes, should it?"

"We'll be back at the library before eight. Timmy and Tommy should be finished their books by then," Amber said confidently. "Let's go."

They marched boldly up the school steps, through the door, and into the main hallway. There was not a soul in sight. Only the continuous murmur from behind closed doors let the girls know that night school was already in progress.

Once clear of the main corridor, they broke into a run, past the office, the supply room and the staff lounge. They bounded up the main stairs to the darkened second floor hallway, then raced to the computer room. A spear of light cut across the floor from beneath the door. Liz swiftly turned the handle. The door swung wide.

"I thought it would still be open," Amber murmured as they entered. "Even the lights are on."

"We'd better hurry in case those night school students come up here," said Amber, pulling off her windbreaker and throwing it over a chair. "Aren't you hot?" she asked, glancing at Liz's wool sweater. "I'm sweating like crazy from all this running around."

"Are you kidding? I've got goosebumps! If we get caught in here, Craig won't be the only one to get kicked out of school. And my father is an educator!" Liz added mournfully.

"Don't think about it," Amber advised, pulling a crumpled piece of foolscap out of the back pocket of her jeans. "I wrote down everything Craig told me about the program." She quickly read over the notations.

"You know," she commented, "this is really clever. We've got to get Craig and Jonathan together. They obviously have brains in common."

"But what do we do now?" asked Liz, pulling up a chair and glancing nervously at the door.

"Load the disk with our English marks on it, reduce all the grades by twenty per cent, and then refile them. With a little luck, the dragon lady will never know."

"Well, hurry," Liz urged.

Just as Amber stretched out her hand to turn on the computer, the fire door slammed at the end of the hall. Someone was coming!

For a split second the girls sat frozen in their seats.

"Hurry!" whispered Liz, coming to her senses. "*Hide!* They must be coming here!"

Amber jumped up, grabbed her jacket, and bumped into Liz.

"*Oomph!*"

"*Watch it!*"

The footsteps were getting nearer. The girls dove for cover behind the filing cabinets in the corner of the room. Frantically, they pressed back into the shadows. The footsteps turned abruptly into the computer room.

Liz held her breath and shut her eyes. Amber

bit her lip then cautiously leaned forward. When she felt Amber's body stiffen beside her, Liz opened her eyes. Chester Mallory was standing in the middle of the room, watching two men who were carrying black attache cases.

Without speaking, the men sat down and switched on two computers. Fascinated, the girls saw them open their cases, remove packages of disks, and load them into the machines. Whatever it was they were doing, it was obvious they knew the routine.

Mallory broke the silence.

"How long are you going to be this time?" he demanded in a surly tone. "It's risky being in here when night school is on. Someone could come in."

Amber stole a glance at Liz, who shrugged her shoulders and shook her head in bewilderment.

"How long do you think you're going to be?" pressed Mallory when the men ignored him. "I told you about all the trouble with these computers — "

"About ten minutes," snapped the man using the machine closest to the door. Although his back was to them, the girls could see he had blond hair, a slight build, and was dressed in a tailored navy sports jacket.

"I still don't understand this," said Mallory peering over the man's shoulder at the computer screen, "but so long as it's money in my pocket, I guess I don't care."

"Just keep that attitude, Mallory. Now why don't you take off and let us work? You'll get paid tomorrow night."

"I'd better," muttered the janitor. "I've risked my job letting you in here."

"You knew the score when you agreed to do it," the other man snapped. "So why don't you shut up and let us get on with it?"

Amber and Liz shifted their gaze to him. He too, had his back to them, but above his heavy shoulders was a shiny, bald head.

Mallory scowled, hesitated, then headed for the door. "Just make sure you turn everything off, and shut the door behind you. I don't want any trouble."

Liz nudged Amber with her foot. There was nothing they could do but wait it out.

For about ten minutes, neither man spoke. They loaded and unloaded several disks. The only sounds were the simultaneous whining of four disk drives, and the occasional keying in of commands.

"That's it," the blond man said at last. He packed the disks back in his case, snapped it shut, then turned off the equipment he had been using. A moment later the bald man did the same.

"Ready?"

"Yeah. Let's go. Get the lights, will you?"

"Right. Mustn't get old Mallory all bent out of shape. We've still got to get in here tomorrow night to copy the last batch of disks."

The lights went out. The door slammed shut.

"Liz?" Amber's voice probed the darkness.

"Here," came the reply. "You okay?"

"Actually, my heart stopped about ten minutes ago," replied Amber, getting to her feet. "Ouch!"

"What happened?"

"I hit my knee on the corner of the filing cabinet. Do you think it's safe to turn on the lights? After all, they were on when we got here."

In reply, the lights flashed on, illuminating Liz slumped against the wall over by the door.

"Geez, you scared me! How'd you get there so fast?"

"I crawled," admitted Liz in a shaky voice. "My legs were too weak for walking."

Amber nodded and sank into a chair.

"Just who were those guys?" she puzzled.

"Beats me. But now we know why Mallory's been such a creep lately," Liz said bitterly. "The mad hacker of Ash Grove has been getting in his way."

"And to think Mallory tried to pin the blame on us," Amber added indignantly. "He's got a lot of nerve!"

"So now what?"

"Let's forget the Belcher curve. That's nickel-dime compared to this."

"Right. Let's get out of here." Liz made a grab for the door handle, and turned it hard. She stopped and looked at her friend.

"Amber," she said tightly, "it's locked. We're trapped in here!"

Chapter 9
To the rescue!

Craig took a deep breath and climbed the front steps of Jonathan's house. He crossed the creaking porch and rang the doorbell. Then he took a step back, shoved his sweating hands into the pockets of his windbreaker, and waited.

About thirty agonizing seconds later, the door swung open. Jonathan stood framed in the doorway.

"Craig! You've got a lot of nerve coming here." Angrily, he started to close the door.

"Jonathan, wait! I've got to talk to you," pleaded Craig.

Jonathan snorted. "After the trouble you and your friends gave me all week? I've got nothing to say to you!"

"Who's there, Jonathan?"

Jonathan hesitated, then turned and called back into the house. "It's okay, Mom. It's just one of the kids from school. I'll be out here for a few minutes."

He stepped outside, closing the door softly behind him.

"Well," he demanded, "what do you want?"

"I've . . . I've come to apologize," Craig said.

"This whole thing with the grade seven projects was all my fault."

"What do you mean, 'all your fault'?"

"I wrote the security program that overrode the grade seven projects . . . " Craig hesitated as Jonathan's face flushed and his thin hands clenched into fists. Resolutely, Craig went on. "And Jane, not Amber and Liz, told the kids you were in the computer room. I . . . uh . . . went along with it. I didn't think it would turn into such a big deal. I'm sorry Jonathan. I'm really sorry."

They stared at each other in silence for a few seconds. Abruptly, Jonathan turned, paced the length of the porch, and slammed his fists down on the railing.

"Great! That's just great! Everyone thinks I screwed up the class projects. Then they call the police who find out I was working on my program for the contest. All thanks to you!"

Craig stepped back, stunned by Jonathan's tirade.

"I didn't even know you were entering the contest," he pleaded. "I was just trying out a security program for the Abacus software. I suppose I was showing off."

"Why?"

Craig shrugged. "I guess I wanted to prove that I'm as good as the computer whiz kids my dad's always talking about."

"Well you sure fixed me. Why didn't you just use your own Abacus?" Jonathan demanded.

"I don't have one. The only Abacus computers outside the factory are the ones being tested at the school."

"Why'd you come and tell me this now?" Jonathan asked suspiciously.

Craig sighed. "I felt bad about it, then Amber and Liz figured it out . . . I guess I'd better go. I'll fix it with Jaws in the morning."

Jonathan watched Craig go down the steps.

"Wait a minute, Craig," he called. "I'll walk part of the way with you. I want to hear how Amber and Liz knew you were the mad hacker . . ."

*   *   *

In the computer room, five minutes had passed, and the girls were still trapped inside.

"We could try yelling," suggested Amber in a dispirited tone. The thrill had gone out of detective work. "Maybe some of the night school people would hear us."

"The way our luck's been going, it would be Mallory and his friends," said Liz. When she had discovered their situation, she had slid to the floor in despair, leaning against the locked door.

"We could be stuck here all night, you know," she added a moment later.

"I know, I know," answered Amber. "It's eight o'clock now," she said, consulting her watch. "In exactly one half hour, either my parents will phone yours, or yours will phone mine. Then, someone will call the library. They'll discover we ditched the twins, were in and out of there in about two seconds, and haven't been seen since."

"Then," said Liz, completing the scenario, "they'll call the police."

Amber groaned.

"What a choice! Mallory or Detective Dexter and his sidekick, Officer Jones, followed directly thereafter, by our hysterical parents."

The conversation depressed them so much that they sat in silence for a little while. Slowly, the minutes ticked by.

* * *

Suddenly Liz looked up.

"Someone's coming!" She jumped to her feet and pressed her ear to the door.

"Are you sure?" Amber joined her. "I don't hear anything."

"Listen!"

Sure enough, there were very faint sounds of someone approaching.

"What if it's Mallory?" Liz whispered.

"No," replied Amber softly, now that she too could hear the noise. "Whoever's coming is trying not to be heard. Mallory is not that subtle."

The footsteps halted on the other side of the door. Slowly, the handle began to turn.

Amber and Liz looked at each other.

"Rats! It's locked," a voice whispered.

"That's Craig!" Amber exclaimed in relief. She pounded on the door. "Craig! Craig! It's us — Liz and Amber! We're locked in here!"

"What are you two doing in there?" came another male voice from the hallway.

"Jonathan?" asked Liz in confusion. "What are you doing here?"

"I asked you first."

"Cut it out," broke in Amber, her confidence restored now that rescue was imminent. "Get us out of here. We'll fill you in on the details later."

"Where's the key?" asked Craig.

The girls pondered this one for a moment.

"You could try Mr. Sharkman's room," suggested Liz, "or the office."

"Why don't we just find Mr. Mallory?" said Jonathan. "He can unlock the door for us."

"No!" cried the girls in unison. "Stay away from Mallory!"

"Why?" demanded Craig.

"Don't argue," ordered Amber frantically. "He's up to something. Just find a key and get us out of here!"

"Oh, all right," Jonathan said from the other side. The girls could hear the boys talking quietly as they went off in search of a key.

"I hope they hurry," Liz said, straightening up. "And I sure hope they don't run into Mallory."

"No kidding," agreed Amber, sitting limply in one of the chairs. "What time is it? I wonder what the twins are doing. I was supposed to look after my brothers, not leave them in the library. If Mallory's shady pals don't kill me, my parents will."

"Amber," Liz said, "just what were those men doing in here?"

"I don't know," Amber replied dispiritedly, her mind still on the twins.

"Think about it," Liz said, shifting to a more comfortable position. "Those guys are businessmen. What reason would they have for sneaking into Ash Grove to use the Abacus?"

Amber looked at her friend with sudden interest. Her eyes narrowed thoughtfully.

"Mallory!" she said triumphantly.

"What about Mallory?" demanded Liz.

"Elementary, my dear Elliot!" Amber exclaimed, jumping up. "Mallory's the key to this whole computer caper. We're just a subplot! There's a real crime going on here — a computer crime — and he's involved. Craig's fiddling with our programs must have scared him silly — police appearing, questioning. That's why he tried to pin the blame on us!"

"To create a diversion," Liz replied shrewdly. "By throwing suspicion on Jonathan, he threw the police off the scent."

"That's it!" Amber agreed, pacing with excitement. "Mallory was desperate. He had to stall the police until tomorrow night, according to what we've heard."

"But why the Abacus?" Liz interrupted.

Amber paused. "That's what we have to figure out."

*   *   *

Jonathan and Craig walked quickly down the darkened corridors of the second floor. Their soft-soled shoes made little noise. Instinctively, they stayed in the shadows, close to the dark grey lockers.

"This is ridiculous," said Craig tensely. "Sneaking around in our own school. I wish we knew why the girls want us to stay away from Mallory."

Jonathan only nodded in reply. Still without speaking, the two boys looked down the dark stairs at the well-lit first floor, where the night classes were still in full swing. Then they hurried down the steps together.

They hesitated at the bottom, scanning the corridors. Empty, except for two men in business suits heading towards the janitor's office. Craig looked after them a moment and frowned.

"Come on," Jonathan urged softly. "What's wrong?"

Craig shrugged. "Nothing. Something about those two looked familiar, that's all."

The boys hurried down the corridor, listening anxiously for any change in the murmurs that came from the adult classes.

"We'll try Jaws' room first," Jonathan said. Craig nodded his agreement.

They reached the room near the end of the corridor. Jonathan turned the handle.

"No good," he muttered. "It's locked."

"What if we tell the secretary in the office that we left our homework in the computer room?" Craig suggested.

"No chance," Jonathan replied. "After what's been going on around here, they'd never let us into there at night."

"I guess it's Mallory then."

Jonathan nodded, and the boys headed back the way they'd come.

"What if we tell him we've locked up our homework?"

"Not after what the girls said. I think our best bet is to make a grab for his keys."

"How?"

"Beats me."

They turned down the corridor towards Mallory's office.

"I guess we wing it."

Outside the storage room which led to the janitor's office, Jonathan peered cautiously around the doorjamb. A shaft of light from Mallory's half-opened door highlighted the darkness, outlining stacked chairs, old bulletin boards, cases of cleaning supplies. Jonathan could hear muffled voices, but could see no one. Taking a deep breath, he slipped into the room, crouched behind a broken desk and motioned Craig to follow.

Together, they crept warily toward Mallory's office door, staying out of the light as best they could. The voices became clearer, but the boys still couldn't see anyone.

"This way," whispered Craig. He wriggled between the utility sink and the huge, wheeled trash cans Mallory used for the school's garbage. Jonathan squirmed after him. Crouched motionless, the two boys had a perfect view into Mallory's office.

The janitor was leaning against the wall, his head just touching a calendar which swung gently back and forth on its nail. A slim, blond man in a navy sports jacket sat in one chair, his fingers slowly stroking his thin moustache. A bald man, suit jacket open to reveal a bulge of

83

stomach above his belt, occupied the chair behind Mallory's desk.

"Now let's get this straight Mallory, once and for all. There's no new deal. You'll get five thousand cash for co-operating — no more, no less. If you think you can bleed us for more money, forget it. We copy the last set of disks tomorrow night. You'll get your money, just like we agreed — tomorrow!"

From their hiding place, the boys heard everything. Craig grabbed Jonathan's arm.

"I know them!" he whispered excitedly. "Those men work for my father!"

Chapter 10
The great escape

Craig's eyes blazed with excitement.

"No wonder the girls warned us about Mallory!" he whispered.

Jonathan nodded, then nudged Craig and pointed to a small table just inside the office door. It was littered with styrofoam cups, an electric kettle, a jar of instant coffee — and Mallory's keys.

"Watch this," Craig said softly. He began crawling stealthily toward the office door. Jonathan held his breath. If any of the men inside glanced in their direction, it would be game over.

Craig crept closer and closer. He went so slowly that the hard grit of the floor seemed to press right through the knees of his pants. But still he kept crawling, determined to get those keys.

The bald man picked up Mallory's phone and began dialing.

Another metre and Craig would be there.

"Hello, Thompson? Rollins. Is tomorrow night all right for our little transaction? No . . . no problem. Everything is smooth at this end. Right."

He hung up.

Craig reached the door. Crouching down out of the path of light, he stretched his hand towards the table. His fingers groped through the litter until they reached what they were searching for.

"*Hey!*" the bald man bellowed. "*You!*"

Craig's hand convulsed over the keys.

"*Run for it!*" Jonathan shouted.

The two boys dashed through the supply room, knocking boxes everywhere. Behind them, they could hear the men crashing about in the darkness, swearing and cursing.

"This way!" shouted Jonathan.

They tore down the hallway, made a dive for the emergency exit, slammed it open. Then they were off into the shadows of the playing field.

Just as they slid down into a small ravine behind the field, the door crashed open again.

"We've got to hide," Jonathan panted.

"Where?" Craig demanded tersely.

"Through here. Follow me!"

With Jonathan in the lead, they groped, panic-stricken, through the small bushes and sumacs until they reached an old storm sewer at the edge of a creek. They plunged inside.

Just moments later, they heard Mallory and the two men on the edge of the field above them.

"I'll bet they're down there!" Mallory said savagely. "Come on. They can't have gone far!"

"This is idiotic," one of the men snapped. "Those kids were probably just fooling around."

"What if they heard something?"

"They wouldn't understand it, even if they did."

"I wish I'd gotten a look at their faces," Mallory snarled. "I'd teach them to play tricks."

"Come on, let's go. We don't want to be seen around here. There's been enough uproar already."

Gradually, the voices faded into the distance. But the boys remained crouched in the storm sewer for several more minutes.

"Ugh!" said Craig when they finally emerged. "My feet are soaked. This'll ruin my shoes."

"Better than getting caught," Jonathan replied matter-of-factly, brushing off his jeans.

"That's for sure."

Still cautious, they followed the creek bank in silence until they were beside the parking lot. There was no one in sight. Crouching down, they slipped between the parked cars and approached the side entrance unseen.

"I suppose we'd better rescue the girls." Craig jingled the keys in his pocket.

"I wouldn't advise leaving them there." Jonathan grinned at the thought. "Our lives wouldn't be worth diddley-squat."

"You're right."

They reentered the school warily. The last thing they wanted was to run into Mallory. As quietly as possible, they sped down the hall, up the dark stairs, and into the deserted second floor corridor.

Craig had the keys out before they'd even reached the computer room.

"Know which one it is?" Jonathan demanded, looking anxiously over his shoulder.

"I'll try them all."

The third key turned the lock.

"It's about time!" Amber flared as they pulled open the door.

"I knew you'd be grateful," said Jonathan.

"Shut up, you two!" Craig hissed. "We've got to get out of here, fast!"

The girls took in the boys' flushed faces and dishevelled clothes, and without another word, followed them down the hallway. They didn't stop running until they were a block away from the school.

"What happened?" demanded Liz, gasping for breath. "Why the panic?"

"I'm not certain." Craig ran his hand through his damp hair. "But if this is what I think it is, we've really stumbled onto something important."

"You two were right," said Jonathan. "Mallory's mixed up in something illegal. We saw him with two men — "

"Baldy and Blondie," Amber interjected. "They were running programs on the Abacus."

"And they locked us in," added Liz.

"You saw them?" Craig demanded. "That's great! You're witnesses then."

"Witnesses to what?" asked Amber. "All we saw were the sides and backs of two guys running programs on the computer."

"It's computer piracy," Jonathan said tersely.

"That's right." Craig's voice was eager. "Those two men work at ET for my dad. They're paying Mallory to let them into Ash Grove to use the Abacus."

"I don't understand," Liz said, frowning. "If they work at ET, why would they come all the way out here to run programs?"

"Copy programs, you mean," Craig replied grimly. "Ash Grove has the only Abacus outside ET itself. The company is spending millions developing the software to go with the computers. With security so tight at the plant, Baldy and Blondie had to come here. They can only copy the programs on another Abacus."

"And then they sell them!" Amber exclaimed in sudden understanding. "They're computer pirates."

"That's what we've been saying," Jonathan pointed out.

"ET's competitors would spend a fortune to get hold of those disks," Craig added.

"And Mallory's helping them!" Amber said in disgust. "That creep. Trying to get us in trouble!"

"Speaking of trouble," Liz said, glancing anxiously at her watch, "it's now exactly 8:46. The library closes in fourteen minutes."

"The twins!" shrieked Amber. "I forgot the twins!"

Without another word, she turned and ran down the sidewalk in the direction of the library. Liz looked at the boys and shrugged.

"We have a domestic crisis. If we survive, we'll meet you tomorrow morning in the cafeteria." Then with a wave, she too disappeared down the sidewalk.

*   *   *

"Hi. It's me."

"Me, who?"

"Amber, you idiot!"

"Well, how was I supposed to know?" demanded Liz on the other end of the line. "You sound like some weirdo."

"So would you, if you were phoning from a linen cupboard."

"What are you doing in the linen cupboard?"

"I'm being punished."

"Your parents put you in the linen cupboard? I don't believe that."

"No, no," replied Amber in exasperation. "I'm being sent to bed early for keeping the twins out late, but I had to call you first to figure out our next move."

"Amber, I am totally confused. You still haven't explained why you are in the linen cupboard."

"Unlike some people I know, I don't have a phone in my bedroom," came the muffled explanation. "I took the upstairs hall phone into the linen cupboard for privacy."

"Did the twins squeal on us?" asked Liz anxiously.

"No, but I had to up the bribe to a chocolate fudge sundae."

Liz groaned "Detective work is getting expensive."

Amber ignored her. "We've got to find a way to catch Mallory in the act."

"Right," Liz agreed. "Got any ideas?"

"No, I was hoping you had."

The line went silent for a few minutes.

"Craig said we were witnesses, right?" said Amber finally.

"Yeah," answered Liz.

"The trouble is, we can't prove what we saw. It's our word against theirs. We need proof."

"And how do we get that?" asked Liz. "We can't show up and politely ask them for the disks."

"Do you still have film in that camera of yours?"

"Yes," Liz replied. "I've got a whole roll."

"Great! Bring it tomorrow night. Oh, oh, somebody's coming! Oh, hi, Mom . . ."

Chapter 11
The mad hacker strikes again

At 8:15, the Ash Grove cafeteria was empty. Liz dumped her books on the nearest table and dropped wearily into a chair.

"I don't see why detective work requires getting up at the crack of dawn," she grumbled sleepily.

"It isn't all that early," Amber grinned. "You should have gone to bed with the twins like I did. Check your watch. Shouldn't the guys be here by now?"

As if on cue, Craig and Jonathan hurried in, pulled out chairs, and sat down beside Liz. Amber leaned on the table in front of them.

"We have a plan," she announced.

"So do we," replied Craig. "Now, here's what we're going to do — "

"Call the police," interjected Liz.

"What for?" demanded Jonathan.

"Crime, police — my mind just automatically links the two together," Liz replied airily.

"No way!" said Craig. "This is our big chance to make up for the trouble we've caused."

"Agreed," Amber declared. "Now here's our plan. We'll go to the computer room tonight at about 7:30, before Blondie and Baldy show up — "

"Right!" Craig interrupted. "Jonathan and I will hide inside. When Mallory lets them in, we'll grab their briefcases and run. The disks inside will be all the proof we need to get Mallory."

"And what are Liz and I supposed to do?" demanded Amber. "Stand by and play cheerleader?"

"Get serious, Amber. This could be dangerous," Jonathan sounded incredulous. "You and Liz can stand guard and let us know when they're coming. If necessary, you can create a diversion."

"The police would make a very nice diversion," Liz commented, "but I suppose that would be too obvious."

"Come on, Liz," said Craig, putting an arm around her shoulder. "Where's your sense of adventure?"

"I don't have one this early in the morning."

"So, we're agreed then?" Craig went on cheerfully.

"Not particularly," Amber snapped.

"Don't worry, Amber. Craig and I know exactly what we have to do. It'll be a breeze. See you later. I've got some homework to finish before classes start." And Jonathan walked off down the hall.

"Me too," Craig said. "We'll meet at 7:15 at the corner of Maple and Broadview. Now don't forget."

"Fine!" Amber hollered after them. "But what about the Belcher curve — you morons."

She sat down in fury. "Did you ever hear anything like it?" she demanded.

"So we go to Plan B," Liz drawled.

"Right," Amber agreed, smiling slowly. "We'll have to save the day, despite those would-be heroes."

"But, of course, Madame Detective," Liz said with a grin. "Now all we have to do is make it to tonight."

* * *

Before long, it was obvious that surviving the day was not going to be as easy as it sounded. Jane Dobbs was feeling left out.

"Amber! Liz!" she called shrilly as soon as the girls reached their locker. "I've been waiting for you." Flanked by several classmates, she approached the two friends.

"Wonderful," muttered Amber.

"I didn't think they cared," agreed Liz.

"This computer stuff has been going on all week," Jane declared, "and you two have been hopping in and out of classes, talking to the police." She paused meaningfully, but neither girl reacted. So she went on. "And we think you're holding out on us."

"That's right," Laurel agreed, while the others nodded. "You two didn't even tell us what the police said."

"We've got a right to know," one of the other students put in. "After all, our projects were lost too."

"The reason we didn't tell you big mouths anything — " Amber began hotly.

"Is because there hasn't been anything to tell," Liz interrupted quickly. Jane stared at her suspiciously. "The police didn't tell us anything. They just asked a bunch of dumb questions about how we lost the programs. In fact," she added in mock gloom, "I got the feeling that the detective thought we'd done it ourselves by mistake. He wasn't sympathetic!" She watched her classmates for their reaction.

"That's right. They probably think it's just a technical problem," Amber added more calmly. "After all, they are test computers. Maybe there's a bug in them or something."

"A big bug," Liz added. Amber elbowed her.

"Well, what about Jonathan?" Jane tried again.

Amber sniffed.

"You might remember we said all along that he had nothing to do with it. If you weren't so eager to spread rumours you could have figured that out for yourself. It isn't that difficult."

Jane glared at them in silence, obviously searching her mind for a new line of attack.

"Well, what about ET?" she insisted finally. "How come they're not buzzing around looking for the problem? After all, the Abacus is their computer." Out of the corner of her eye, she suddenly spotted Craig approaching his locker.

"Hey Craig!" she called, rounding eagerly on her new victim. "You've been awfully busy lately . . ."

She stalked off in his direction. The other students followed.

Angrily, Amber pulled their locker open while Liz stared after Jane.

"I wish someone would feed her into the Abacus," Amber muttered.

"Then there'd really be a bug in the system," laughed Liz. "Amber, I think we'd better rescue Craig from our dear Ms. Dobbs. She's got him backed against the lockers."

"I suppose we have to," Amber sighed. "If Motormouth finds out about our plans, the bad guys will get away for sure." She slammed the door shut.

" . . . and what I want to know," Jane was saying, her face pushed close to Craig's, "is how come ET doesn't have technicians here, right now, checking this out? What does your father have to say about this?"

"Nothing," Craig said angrily. "Jane, back off! My dad doesn't know anything about it."

"He *doesn't*?" Jane stepped back in amazement. "*Well!* No wonder nothing is getting done. I'm going right now to tell Mr. Sharkman he'd better call your father. *I* think he'll be furious that no one has told him about what's happened!"

She turned and marched off down the hall, smiling in triumph.

"Too late," Liz observed.

"Here we go again," Amber agreed.

Craig stared after her glumly. "I bet she'll call Dad herself, if Jaws won't."

"Never mind," Amber said consolingly. "Once we've nabbed the bad guys, everything will be fine."

"If we make it through Miss Belcher's class," Liz remarked.

As if emphasizing her words, the bell for the first period shrilled through the halls.

* * *

"Settle down, class," Miss Belcher said loudly. "We'll begin today with our new text, *Great Expectations*, by Charles Dickens. Amber, in light of your rather mediocre performance on the last class assignment" — she paused to give Amber a significant stare — "it might be appropriate for you to start the reading."

Flushing, Amber stood up, thumbed to the correct page, and opened her mouth to begin. But a tap at the classroom door followed by the appearance of Mr. Sharkman put a sudden end to her recitation.

"Oh, Mr. Sharkman," cooed Miss Belcher. "Are you bringing us the results of our first computerized English test?"

"Right here." Mr. Sharkman handed her some sheets of computer printout. "And, if I may say so, your students should all be congratulated. These grades are exemplary."

"I beg your pardon?"

"Perhaps I shouldn't have glanced at them, but I am interested in anything to do with the Abacus. There was not a single grade lower than 82."

The students cheered. Amber and Liz exchanged glances, trying not to laugh. A red-faced Craig was apparently absorbed in the first page of *Great Expectations*.

"Mr. Sharkman" — Miss Belcher's voice lowered ominously — "I would hate to imply that your precious Abacus made an error, but I can assure you that *this* class is incapable of grades like that."

"Miss Belcher, I took these directly from the Abacus. There is no mistake."

There was an uncomfortable silence. Amber unobtrusively slid back down into her seat. Craig stared fixedly at his book. Liz studied a poster of Shakespeare on the wall with great intensity. Miss Belcher continued to examine the offending printout.

"Did you happen to read this small footnote at the bottom, Mr. Sharkman?"

"And what footnote is that, Miss Belcher?"

"The Mad Hacker strikes again!"

The class was in an uproar. Miss Belcher turned, marched to her desk, and sat down. She stared coldly at the class until the silence was absolute. Mr. Sharkman cleared his throat, muttered something about double-checking the Abacus, and disappeared.

"Amber!" Miss Belcher commanded sharply. Amber jumped in her seat. "Would you be so kind as to go down to the office, and ask the secretary for the printouts of the tests I took the precaution of having made last week?"

"Yes ma'am," Amber said nervously, rising from her seat.

"I'll help her." Liz darted through the door before Miss Belcher could object.

"Whew," Amber said once they were out in the hall. "The only thing missing was smoke."

"No kidding!" Liz giggled in relief.

"Look," Amber said as they approached the office. Mallory was inside talking heatedly with the secretary.

"How should I know where I lost them?" he was saying. "If I knew where I'd lost my keys, I'd be able to find them, wouldn't I?"

"Well, do you have a spare set?" Miss Kimble's face was hot with anger.

"Yeah, and it's a good thing for this school that I do," Mallory growled. "You're going to have to get another set made for me though."

Liz and Amber intently studied the bulletin board just inside the door.

"I'll be with you girls in a minute," Miss Kimble called. "I have to fill out a requisition for Mr. Mallory. It seems he's lost his keys."

"Fine. No rush," Amber's tone was bright. She smiled hesitantly at Mallory. "Nice day," she offered.

Mallory eyed her suspiciously, then turned back to the secretary. "Hurry up, will you?"

"Yes, yes, Mr. Mallory," Miss Kimble replied sharply, "but I see no reason to be so rude."

"It's part of his charm," Amber muttered.

Liz jabbed her in the ribs. "Look who's coming."

Amber turned to see Ernest Jones holding the door open for Detective Dexter and the principal, Mr. Cline. The principal led the detective into his office and closed the door, leaving Officer Jones outside. The policeman looked around, saw Liz, and nodded in recognition.

"Don't you want to go over and say hello?" teased Amber.

"Shut up, Amber," said Liz, smiling all the while at the young officer.

Suddenly, Mallory, his eyes down, pushed past the girls and out of the office.

"Honestly," Miss Kimble said, "that man is unbearable. Now, what can I do for you girls?"

"Miss Belcher sent us for the English tests she left here last week," Amber said.

"Oh, yes. I have them here under the counter. Miss Belcher certainly doesn't trust those computers."

She handed a pile of papers to Amber. Liz absentmindedly said thanks to Miss Kimble, and walked ahead of her friend into the hallway. Amber shrugged and followed after her.

"You could help," she said. But Liz was standing in the middle of the corridor, obviously deep in thought.

"What? Oh yeah. Say Amber, could you take them back? I just thought of something I forgot . . ."

"*Liz!*"

But Liz had already left, running quickly down the hall in the direction of their locker.

"This case is getting to her." Amber adjusted the papers in her arms and headed back toward Miss Belcher's classroom.

Liz spun the combination to her locker and glanced furtively down the hall. No one was watching. She yanked open the metal door and scrounged in the clutter for pen and paper. Once found, she chewed the end of the pen for a moment, then hastily scribbled a few sentences.

"This should do it." She checked her watch. Five minutes before the bell would ring to signal the end of the period. Quickly, she pushed her locker shut and hurried back down the hall toward the office. So far, so good. Liz hesitated a moment outside, then took a deep breath and went in.

"Miss Kimble," she said bravely.

"Oh yes, Liz. Did you forget something?"

"No . . . well, yes. I noticed that Officer Jones isn't here right now."

"No. I believe he's in the office. Should I call him?"

"Oh no," Liz said hastily. "I'm a friend of . . . of his sister, and she's given me a note. Could you give this to him, please?" She thrust the folded paper across the counter to the secretary.

"Of course, Liz. No problem at all."

"That's what I'm hoping," Liz said under her breath, as she scurried out of the office and back toward Miss Belcher's class.

The bell rang just as she reached the door. Instead of entering and offering explanations, Liz waited outside. Amber appeared a minute later carrying all their books.

"Here," she said, dropping part of the pile into Liz's arms.

"Did Miss Belcher notice that I didn't come back?"

"No. I don't think she even noticed that I came back. She spent the rest of the period lecturing about how all the great works of literature were *not* written on computers. I thought poor Craig was going to choke."

Liz laughed. "It must have been awful for him."

"By the way," Amber said, "where did you take off to?"

"I uh . . . I had to see someone."

"Who?"

The bell for the beginning of the next period rang.

"We have to get moving," Liz said with obvious relief. "Besides, he'd left."

"Who had left? Liz — "

But Liz had already gone into their next class.

Chapter 12
A picture is worth a thousand words

"What's taking so long?" Amber asked anxiously, looking out at the parking lot.

"For Pete's sake, there must be twenty keys here," answered Craig, fumbling with the ring he'd taken from Mallory's office the night before.

"It's a good thing you held on to those," commented Liz. "Otherwise, we wouldn't be able to get into the school tonight."

"That's right," agreed Jonathan. "There's no night school on Fridays." He looked nervously over his shoulder. The parking lot was empty except for a shadowy pickup truck. He was sure it was Mallory's. Knowing the janitor was already in the school made him shiver underneath his thin jacket.

"Got it!" Craig exclaimed triumphantly. He held open the door while the others filed by him silently. He followed, carefully closing the door behind him.

"It sure is spooky in here," whispered Liz. "Hardly any lights are on." Her eyes were as big as saucers.

"Especially now that Mallory is here too," commented Jonathan.

"He is? How do you know?" Amber demanded.

"I'm sure that's his truck parked outside."

"Why didn't you tell us before?" asked Craig.

"I didn't want to make you nervous."

"Thanks a lot," said Amber sarcastically.

"Hadn't we better get going?" interrupted Liz. "We're right around the corner from Mallory's office."

"Right," Craig said.

The four detectives hurried up the end staircase and crept along the darkened upper hall to the computer room.

"Do you remember which key unlocks the door?" asked Jonathan.

"I think it's this gold one," replied Craig, pushing it into the lock. He turned the handle. The door swung open noiselessly.

"All right," said Amber. "In you go."

"But first," said Liz, extending her opened hand, "give me the keys."

"What?" Jonathan and Craig exclaimed in unison.

"That's right," said Liz. "We're going to lock you in."

"I don't remember that being part of the plan," argued Craig.

"Look," explained Amber, "if Mallory comes along and finds this door open, he'll smell a rat for sure."

"She's right," admitted Jonathan. "If we're

going to catch those guys, we can't afford to let Mallory suspect anything."

Reluctantly, Craig handed over the keys. Then he and Jonathan moved inside the unlit computer room.

"Don't worry boys," teased Liz. "We'll come back for you — eventually." She giggled and shut the door.

Clutching the keys firmly so they wouldn't jangle, Liz followed Amber to the girls' washroom on the other side of the hall. They stationed themselves inside to wait.

"Did you remember your camera?" Amber asked softly.

"Right here." Liz removed a little pocket camera from her jacket. "I didn't want the boys to see it."

Amber held the washroom door open a crack, and peered down the hallway. "Shh!" she cautioned. "I think I hear something."

A few seconds later, Mallory and the two men from Eastern Technology appeared at the top of the main stairway. Amber watched as the janitor unlocked the computer room door and let them in. A shaft of light appeared from the doorway. Amber hoped the boys were well concealed.

"Will you please tell me what's going on? I can't see a thing." Liz impatiently pulled at Amber's sleeve.

"They're in there now," whispered Amber in reply. "Wait a minute — I think Mallory's leaving. Yes, there he goes, down the stairs." She closed the door softly and retreated into the washroom.

"We'll have to wait a few minutes. We want to make sure we catch them copying the disks."

"Right." Liz consulted the luminous dial of her watch. "It's 7:45. We'll move in at 7:47. Here." She passed Amber the ring of keys. "Have you got a pocket big enough for these? I'm going to need both hands free."

Amber shoved them into the kangaroo pocket of her jacket.

"All set."

"Okay," Liz checked her watch again. "It's time to go."

They left their hiding place and crept toward the computer room.

"I'm scared," confessed Amber in a whisper.

"Me too."

They were only about a metre from the door now. It was partially open.

"Okay, Liz. Do your stuff." Amber leaped forward and threw open the door.

"Smile for the birdie!" she yelled at the two men sitting in front of the Abacus equipment.

Their horrified faces were frozen forever as Liz quickly snapped the picture.

"Got it!" she hollered. "Let's get out of here!"

The two girls turned and ran for the main staircase, spurred on by the enraged shouts of the men behind them.

"*Stop!*"

"*What do you think you're doing!*"

As they reached the top of the staircase, Amber and Liz could hear the pounding footsteps of Baldy and Blondie catching up to them.

"Quick! Down here," called Amber. They flew down the steps and into the main hall.

"Not that way! Mallory's office is down there!"

"Too late now," panted Amber. "They're right behind us."

They raced down the hall toward the parking lot exit. With only a short distance to go, Mallory suddenly appeared between the double doors ahead of them.

"The gym door!" yelled Amber. They swung around and raced down the short hallway between the gym and Mallory's office.

"It's locked!" screamed Liz, pushing against the exit in a panic. "We can't get out!"

"Back the way we came!"

They sped back to the main hallway, just as Baldy and Blondie burst from the centre staircase.

"Grab them!" bellowed Baldy.

"We're trapped," groaned Liz.

The girls stood rigid with terror as Mallory advanced on them from one end of the hallway and the computer thieves from the other.

"We've got you now," hissed Mallory. "I knew it had to be you two. You took my keys too, didn't you?" He stalked toward them menacingly. "You'll pay for this."

The girls cowered against the wall.

"You were right, Liz," whispered Amber shakily. "We should have called the police."

"Mallory," shouted Blondie, "grab the kid with the camera!"

Liz tried to burrow into the locker behind her.

"Don't you lay a finger on those girls, Mallory!" rang out a familiar voice. Mr. Eugene Sharkman, flanked by Detective Dexter and Mr. Cline, strode into the hallway.

"Hands up and against the wall!" barked Detective Dexter, giving Baldy a shove. "You too!" He pointed his gun at Blondie.

"Watch out! Mallory's getting away!" shouted Liz.

The janitor had bolted for the parking lot exit. He slammed open the outer door and ran straight into the arms of Officer Jones and Craig's father. The two men marched him back.

"Mallory, explain yourself," the principal ordered sharply.

Mallory's eyes narrowed.

"These men," he nodded in the direction of Baldy and Blondie, "told me they were special technicians — here to fix the Abacus."

"On a Friday night?"

"He's lying!" Amber's accusation rang out loud and clear.

"That's right," confirmed Liz. "Those men are paying Mallory to let them into the computer room. They're copying stolen programs on the Abacus."

"And we've got the disks to prove it!" announced Craig as he and Jonathan raced onto the scene, carrying a handful of black disks.

"Craig!" Robert Nicholson exclaimed. "What are you doing here?"

"Retrieving the disks stolen from ET," he said.

"Those disks don't prove anything," Blondie said. "It's a kid's word against ours."

"But a picture is worth a thousand words!" declared Liz, holding up her camera with a flourish.

"You girls took a photograph of these men using the Abacus?" asked Mr. Nicholson incredulously.

"That's right." Liz's pride was obvious in her voice.

"I've got to hand it to you," said Mr. Nicholson, looking keenly at his son and his three friends. "We've suspected something like this was going on, but we couldn't be sure. How did you four discover what these men were doing?"

"It's . . . it's kind of complicated, Dad," Craig stammered.

"It was Amber and Liz — they have a knack for mysteries," put in Jonathan.

"I see," replied Mr. Nicholson. "I'm going to want to hear all about it. But in the meantime" — he turned to confront his two employees — "this type of crime will not be tolerated. I can promise you that Eastern Technology will prosecute you both to the limit."

"Don't kid yourself, Nicholson. That won't change anything," sneered Baldy. "If we can crack your security, anyone can."

"Maybe not, Dad." Craig sounded eager. "I've been working on a new security system for the Abacus."

Mr. Nicholson looked at his son intently.

"Can you show me?"

Aware of Jaws' shrewd eyes, Craig took a deep breath before speaking. "It's already working. I used it to lock the grade seven programs."

"Well, all this is beyond me," interjected Detective Dexter as he finished handcuffing the three men. "Jones and I will run these men down to the station."

"I'll come with you and press charges on the school's behalf," said Mr. Cline.

"And I'll join you later," added Mr. Nicholson, "after I see this security program of Craig's. I'll bring the disks with me then."

"Fine," said Detective Dexter. He turned to Liz. "I'll need that camera of yours, young lady. By the way, slipping this note to Officer Jones was very wise. You kids could have been badly hurt."

Amber took the note the detective held out, and read aloud:

The mad hacker of Ash Grove needs your help! The Computer Pirates will strike tonight. Be at the school at 8 p.m.
A Friend of ET.

Liz flushed as Amber eyed her knowingly.

"All right, partner," Amber said, giving her friend a hug.

They all watched as Detective Dexter shepherded the grimfaced trio of prisoners toward the exit, accompanied by Officer Jones and Mr. Cline.

Jaws laid a hand on Craig's shoulder.

"Well, well, Craig. So you're the mad hacker of Ash Grove."

"Yes, sir," Craig looked up at Mr. Sharkman sheepishly.

"We'll talk about it later. I think your father would like to see that security program." He led the way upstairs to the computer room.

"There's the rest of your evidence, Mr. Nicholson." Jonathan pointed to the open attache cases on the floor. They still contained about a dozen disks.

"Thank goodness," said Mr. Nicholson, examining the contents. "Your detective work has saved Eastern Technology a small fortune." He closed the two cases and put them beside the door. "Now, Craig, let's see this security system."

Efficiently, Craig took the appropriate disk from the school files and loaded it.

"This is how it works," he said, and rapidly keyed in a series of commands. Amber and Liz peered over his shoulder at the monitor.

"Do you understand this?" Liz whispered.

"I haven't got a clue," replied Amber.

"Some detective you turned out to be." The two girls shrugged their shoulders.

" . . . and here come the grade seven programs."

"I'm impressed, Craig," said Mr. Nicholson, with pride in his voice.

Craig's face lit up.

"I think we can count this as your class project," added Mr. Sharkman. "It's definitely worth an A. It had me completely baffled."

"Dad," said Craig, "Jonathan has a program for the Abacus I think you should see. He's really the best programmer in the school."

111

"In grade eight, anyway," Jonathan said with a grin.

"Why don't you enter it in ET's software contest?" asked Mr. Nicholson.

"I'd like to sir," replied Jonathan shyly. "But I need to work on it some more."

"Eugene," Mr. Nicholson said, "do you think you could allow this boy extra time on the Abacus?"

Jaws smiled and nodded his agreement.

"I am so relieved that we didn't lose *Whodunnit* after all this," Liz put in.

"What's *Whodunnit*?" asked Mr. Nicholson.

"Oh," exclaimed Amber brightly, "it's this great program Liz and I wrote — at least it will be, when we can get Aunt Agatha to stop killing the butler . . ."

Epilogue

"Double fudge," Timmy told the waitress. "It's okay — my sister's paying."

"No nuts, lots of whipped cream," added Tommy, "and a cherry!"

"You'll both get fat," Amber told them, leaning back in the booth at the Ice Cream Emporium.

"That's right," agreed Liz. "And, unlike us, you won't be going to camp to work it all off — swimming, sailing, back to nature . . . "

"I still can't believe it," Amber replied. "When Mr. Nicholson called this morning to offer the four of us two free weeks at ET's computer camp, I just about choked on my cornflakes! Timmy . . . sit down!"

"I was just trying to see if our sundaes were coming," Timmy said reproachfully, as Liz hauled him back into his seat.

"It'll be a lot more relaxing than last week, that's for sure," Liz said.

"It should be . . . " agreed Amber, her voice trailing off. The two friends' eyes met across the table. They smiled knowingly.

"But who knows what might happen," observed Liz, "when the dynamic duo are on the scene!"

Author, creative writing teacher and freelance writer **Anne Stephenson** finds plenty of raw material right at home. With two teenagers and a pair of cats underfoot, there's no end to life's little mysteries. If anyone knows where her rechargeable batteries are, please call. She's fading fast.

After living in several Canadian and U.S. cities, **Susan Brown** now makes her home in Seattle with her husband, three children and dog. When not working on a script or book, she teaches writing and works on curriculum and technology committees for the school district. She also gardens, reads, and contemplates the ongoing chaos of her house.